PROMISE

Copyright © 2015 Judy Young

Library of Congress Cataloging-in-Publication Data
Young, Judy, 1956-
Promise / written by Judy Young.
pages cm
Summary: Eleven-year-old Kaden, a boy who lives with his grandmother outside the small town of Promise, learns, just when he is starting middle school, that the father he has never known was released from prison.
ISBN 978-1-58536-914-0 (hard cover : alk. paper) -- ISBN 978-1-58536-915-7 (paper back : alk. paper)
[1. Conduct of life--Fiction. 2. Fathers and sons--Fiction. 3. Ex-convicts--Fiction. 4. Middle schools--Fiction. 5. Schools--Fiction. 6. Grandmothers--Fiction. 7. Crows as pets--Fiction.] I. Title.
PZ7.Y8664Pro 2015
[Fic]--dc23
2015003515

ISBN 978-1-58536-914-0 (case)
1 3 5 7 9 10 8 6 4 2

ISBN 978-1-58536-915-7
1 3 5 7 9 10 8 6 4 2

Printed in the United States.

Sleeping Bear Press™

2395 South Huron Parkway, Suite 200
Ann Arbor, MI 48104

© 2015 Sleeping Bear Press
visit us at sleepingbearpress.com

A NOVEL BY JUDY YOUNG

PROMISE

PUBLISHED BY SLEEPING BEAR PRESS

For Ross
and his brethren, the crow.
Love, Judy

Any day with a crow in it is full of promise.

—*Crows*, Candace Savage

Friday, August 26

CHAPTER ONE

THE FIRE TOWER

If Kaden had gotten the dog he wanted for his eleventh birthday, it would have barked when the man walked up the narrow path from the road. The man would have wondered how a dog got trapped in the top of an abandoned fire tower. He would have tried to rescue it, and Kaden's secret hiding spot would have been discovered instantly. But the man took no notice of a crow cawing incessantly from the window of the fire tower. Kubla was much better than a watchdog if you really wanted no one to notice you. And that was exactly what Kaden wanted. No one to notice.

Kaden should have easily gone through life unnoticed. He was very average. Average height and weight. Unnoticeable brown hair and eyes. Made average grades. But in the small town of Promise, Kaden felt he stood out like a crow against snow. He was the kid whose father was in prison.

When Kaden first heard the vehicle, he picked up the binoculars. Not many cars turned onto the rutted, nearly undriveable dirt road leading up to the fire tower. On the first warm days of spring or when the color changed in the fall, a few hikers might come from Chapston City, forty miles to the north. They would park at the log barricade and wander up the weedy path to the tower. There, they'd be disappointed to discover the bottom set of stairs was gone.

But this was a scorching August Friday. Hikers rarely came in the summer, discouraged not only by the heat but also by ticks and jungles of poison ivy. Kaden put the binoculars to his eyes. He focused on the spot where a small piece of road showed through the trees. Kubla sat on his shoulder. The vehicle soon passed through the open spot: an old white pickup with a big plastic cargo carrier taking up most of the bed.

When the truck disappeared under layers of leaves, Kaden sat down out of sight from anyone below and waited. Kubla waited, too, chattering in Kaden's ear and pulling at strands of his hair. He pestered Kaden whenever he wanted to play, but now Kaden gently pushed the bird off his shoulder. It wasn't long before the truck pulled up at the log barricade. Music drifted from its open windows. Then the engine turned off and the music quit. A door squeaked open and slammed shut. There was no talking.

Just one hiker, Kaden thought. He was tempted to take a quick peek but was afraid he'd be seen. People always looked up when they first approached the fire tower.

Kubla darted out one of the paneless windows, making a racket of harsh warning caws. Kaden knew the hiker was making the usual inspection of the tower and surrounding area. When Kubla perched on his favorite limb near the edge of the clearing and quieted to just a few grunts, Kaden knew the hiker was heading back toward the truck.

Kaden quietly peeked out. A man in blue jeans, a T-shirt, and a cowboy hat was stepping over the log barricade, his back to the tower. He didn't look like the typical hiker. No daypack. No canteen hanging from his belt.

Kaden ducked back out of sight until he heard the truck start up. Once again, he picked up the binoculars. In the summer it was hard, but if he got at just the right angle, he could see where the dirt road met the main road. Kaden wanted to see which way the truck turned.

If the truck turned right, it would go around the bend past the five stone cabins where Kaden lived with Gram. Disappointed hikers frequently stopped there to ask where the trailhead was. Gram always had a grumpy lecture waiting for Kaden if hikers stopped.

"A worthless lot," she'd say. "They've got too much time on their hands if they can just go tromping aimlessly through the woods all day. What they need are jobs, but not one even offered to help. It's obvious the place could use some fixin' up."

Not that Gram would accept help from strangers, and she certainly wouldn't pay anyone. She had Kaden, and when hikers bothered Gram, Kaden could expect extra chores to satisfy Gram's fight against laziness.

Kaden kept his binoculars aimed at the little spot of road. If the truck turned left, it would curve down the hill and drive by Emmett's. Emmett Adams was the only other person who lived this side of Promise. You couldn't see his house from the cabins, but the old man was their only neighbor.

Unlike Gram, Emmett enjoyed company and had hand-painted signs lined up by the road inviting people to stop. One had a horse's head with a cartoon bubble saying "Be Neigh . . . borly! Pull on in and have a chat." Another had a dog saying "Come on in, I don't bite." On a third was a stick figure in a T-shirt, shorts, and big hiking boots saying

"Hike on in—FREE DRINKS." Not many stopped but when someone did, Emmett loved it.

"There's no hiking trail at the tower," Emmett would say, "but there's the promise of a good time right down the hill."

The hikers would politely chuckle at his lame joke but Emmett knew the hikers were good for business at the Big Apple Grocery Store and Pillie's Purple Cow.

Now Kaden saw the truck slow to a stop at the main road.

"Good, he turned left," Kaden told Kubla, who had flown back to the tower and was now strutting around the floor, proud he had run off another intruder. "Gram's been grouchy enough lately without strangers irritating her." Even as he said this, he wasn't convinced the man in the white truck was really a stranger, though.

Kaden put down the binoculars and looked absently at the vast view of the late summer forest that spread in all directions below him. Normally, he would have been dreading returning to school. This year should have been especially worrisome. He would be starting middle school. But today, the last Friday of summer vacation, all Kaden could think about was the letter. It had been four days since the letter arrived. Four days of being able to think of nothing else.

Monday, August 22

CHAPTER TWO

FoUR DAYS EARLIER

"Walk down to Emmett's and see if we got any mail over the weekend," Gram said after lunch.

Their mailbox was in front of Emmett's, the result of one of Gram's irrational fights. Gram didn't want her mailbox on the side of the road. It was constantly being bashed in by teenagers with baseball bats. So she moved the mailbox next to her porch steps. But Mr. Schmerz, the mailman, refused to pull through the circle drive that curved in front of the cabins. A feud started between Gram and Mr. Schmerz. Knowing Gram could not win against the U.S. Postal Service, Emmett stepped in with a solution. Gram's mail would be delivered at Emmett's. Emmett had welded odd pieces of heavy steel from old cars and tractors around his mailbox. It looked like a rusty piece of abstract art. Emmett called it the arm breaker and boasted he was never awakened by the sound of a bat hitting metal.

"It's too hot and we never get anything anyway," Kaden told Gram. "Besides, you haven't seen Emmett for a couple of days."

If there was any mail, Emmett would take an evening stroll to deliver it to Gram's door. Emmett was the only company Gram ever had.

"Well, you can't be loafing around here all day," Gram replied. "There's wash to hang out."

So instead of mail duty, Kaden got laundry duty. And Gram didn't believe in dryers.

"Why pay for something the sun can do for free?" Gram said.

Sweating out in the hot sun, Kaden hung shirts and pants on the clothesline. When the line could hold no more, he carried the rest to the porch, where he draped socks and underwear over the rails. Then he quickly went inside, grabbed a book, and spent the rest of the afternoon reading in the shade of the porch. He knew Gram wouldn't interrupt reading with more chores. Reading was about the only thing she deemed more important.

Just before supper, Gram called out, "Those clothes ought to be dry by now."

Kaden went to the clothesline with two baskets, one for Gram's clothes, one for his. When the clothesline was empty, he moved to the porch. He rolled two socks together and tossed them into his basket. Gram sat opposite him on the old metal glider, husking corn. She looked at the spine of the book sitting next to her.

"I see you had letter 'G' out again. Can't you read about anything besides Genghis Khan?" Gram asked.

Kaden knew Gram would quiz him and had an answer ready. "As a matter of fact, I read about gingko. It's a tree that grows in China and has leaves like little fans. It says the fruit smells putrid."

Kaden pictured hurling a gingko fruit at Luke when school started, but he knew even if he had one, he'd never have the guts to plaster Luke with it. As Kaden rolled another ball of socks, Emmett sauntered up the circle drive.

"Mail call," Emmett announced.

Climbing the squeaky porch steps, Emmett shoved a flyer announcing back-to-school sales into Kaden's hands.

"Look through this and circle what you'll need," he stated. Then he handed Kaden another envelope. "This one's from the school. Probably has your class schedule in it."

Emmett stepped past Kaden and handed Gram an envelope.

"It's from the Center," he whispered, but Kaden heard anyway.

Gram opened the letter and quickly read the contents to herself.

"Is it from Dad?" Kaden asked. "What's it say?"

"Nothing important," Gram answered. She got up and went in the cabin. Kaden heard her dresser drawer being pulled open, then closed shut.

"You need any squash, Emmett?" Gram said when she returned.

"I could do with a couple," Emmett answered.

Kaden knew if the letter were nothing important, Gram would have just thrown it away. He also knew Emmett didn't need any vegetables. He had his own garden behind his shop. Gram always used the vegetable garden as a chance to talk to Emmett in private, and the only time she talked in private was when something was important.

"I'll help," Kaden volunteered, hoping to hear the conversation.

"No," Gram said, "go put away your clothes and wash up for supper."

Kaden picked up his laundry basket and jumped off the

porch. The porch was part of Gram's cabin, not his. Gram's was Cabin Three, the biggest of the five. It was the only one with two rooms, if not counting the bathroom. It was also the only cabin with three windows, one on each side of the front door and one in back, in Gram's bedroom.

The front room was both living room and kitchen. A little table with a bright yellow tablecloth was pushed against the wall under the kitchen window. The living room had an easy chair, a couch, and a bookcase filled with a set of old encyclopedias. Two intercoms sat on the top of the bookcase, both with a dot of red light shining.

Kaden carried his clothes to the cabin next door. That was his cabin. Cabin Two. There was no porch on Kaden's cabin, and except for the small bathroom that had only a toilet and a sink, Kaden's cabin had only one room and one window. Kaden put the flyer and his schedule on his desk next to another set of intercoms. Both red lights on these intercoms were also lit.

When Kaden turned ten, Gram let him move into Cabin Two. Until then he had slept on the hide-a-bed couch in Gram's cabin. But part of the deal was there would be two sets of intercoms and they would both be permanently left on. From one, Kaden could always hear Gram as she puttered about in her living room–kitchen. From the other,

Gram could always hear Kaden, and the two could talk to each other just like people talking from two different rooms in a normal house.

Kaden turned up the volume on one of the intercoms and put his ear close. Other than the hum of Gram's fan, there was no sound. Rushing back to Gram's cabin, he quietly entered her room and opened the dresser drawer. There lay the opened envelope. It was addressed to Gram. In the upper left-hand corner, in scrawly handwriting, it said, *Dennis McCrory, #27665*. Below that was the preprinted return address of the Chapston City State Correctional Center.

Kaden pulled the letter out of the envelope but was only able to read the first few words before he heard the porch steps squeak. He stuffed the letter in the envelope, put it back in the dresser, and quietly pushed the drawer shut. Darting from the room, Kaden plopped into the easy chair and watched through the screen door as Gram waved good-bye to Emmett from the top of the porch steps.

"What did the letter say?" Kaden asked again when Gram came in.

"Nothing that concerns you," Gram said.

"But—" When Kaden started to protest, Gram interrupted.

"I sure wish this heat wave would break," she said, and

Kaden knew there would be no more discussion about the letter.

After dinner, Kaden automatically went to the sink and turned on the water. Unless he was sick, there was no getting around washing the dishes every evening. The screen door banged shut behind him and the springs on the porch chair moaned as Gram sat down. Soon Gram's humming came through the kitchen window. She did that when something weighed on her mind. Not a musical hum. More of a grumbly, muttering hum that almost sounded like words. A blurring of "I don't know" and "maybe if," which slid into low guttural gratings. It reminded Kaden of Kubla's mutterings.

The grumbling hum stopped and the porch steps squeaked. Footsteps crunched across the gravel of the circle drive. Kaden looked out the window and saw Gram walking away from the cabin. Quickly, he sneaked back to Gram's bedroom. He knew it was wrong but he wanted to know what the letter said. After all, it was from his father. He quietly opened the drawer, but the letter was gone.

Kaden sighed and went back to the dishes. He knew the letter was curling to ash in the stone fireplace that sat like a monument on the crescent-shaped lawn. That was the place all letters went that had Chapston City State Correctional Center in the upper left-hand corner. But Kaden had seen some of the words in this letter and they were distinctly burned into his mind.

> *Dear Mom,*
> *It's been almost eight years now and my parole will be coming up. There's a few things I got to take care of first, but I should be at the cabins around...*

Kaden had not had time to read the rest.

Friday, August 26

CHAPTER THREE

THE TRUCK

Now, four days after reading part of his father's letter, Kaden stood in the fire tower, binoculars hanging around his neck. He stared absently toward the spot where he saw the white truck turn left. So much was going through his mind, one thought kept interrupting another.

"It wasn't Dad," he told Kubla. "Dad would know to turn right."

Even though he said the words aloud, he didn't believe them. Deep in his gut, he knew the man was his father, and the thought made him both excited and apprehensive.

"Why would he turn left?" he said aloud again. He frequently talked to the bird and Kubla always tilted his head like an attentive listener. "Maybe he already went home. Maybe Gram told him where I was and he came looking for me and now he's heading back to town. What do you think, Kubla? Do you think I should have called down to him?"

Kaden sat down heavily. There was no doubt in his mind. It was what he had waited for for years and worried about for years. His dad was out of prison.

For more than an hour Kaden sat on the floor of the fire tower. Kubla jumped on his shoulder, pulled at his hair, hopped to the floor, untied Kaden's shoes. The bird went through his entire repertoire of attention-getting antics but Kaden didn't seem to notice. Finally determining Kaden was in no mood to play, Kubla settled in Kaden's lap. Kaden absently smoothed the bird's black feathers. The rhythm of cicadas chirping in the heat was hypnotizing. The crow gurgled softly. A fly buzzed in the corner. Kaden's eyes became heavy and his head drooped to his chest.

Kubla heard it first. As he sprang from Kaden's lap, cawing raucously, Kaden startled awake. The bird darted through the window as the sound of a vehicle reached Kaden's ears.

"Dad's back!" Kaden said as he grabbed the binoculars,

his heart racing. Holding his breath, he once again kept his eyes glued to the spot where the trees parted. When he saw a truck through the gap, he lowered the glasses, let out a long breath, and wiped the sweat off his forehead.

Kaden opened the trapdoor on the floor, climbed down a flight of metal stairs, and stopped on the top landing. Standing in full view, he looked toward the log barricade just as the truck pulled up. A blue truck. Emmett's truck.

"Hi, Emmett!" Kaden yelled down as Emmett walked up the path. "What's up?"

"You're up," Emmett hollered. Kaden grinned. The two always said the same thing whenever Emmett came to the fire tower. "But you need to come down," Emmett continued. "Gram sent me."

There was only one time Kaden didn't get home from the tower by suppertime. A furious Gram had walked to Emmett's and sent him to collect Kaden. Kaden had been grounded from the tower for a month, and during that time, Kubla almost forgot who he was.

Kaden turned and hurried back up into the tower cabin, reprimanding himself for falling asleep and wondering how late it was. He opened the lid to a metal chest bolted to the wall and put the binoculars inside. Then he grabbed a coil of rope that hung from a peg. A baseball-size rock with a hole all the way through it hung from the end. Kaden clattered down the nine flights of stairs to the last landing, twenty feet above the ground. He sat down on the landing, feet dangling over the edge, and wrapped the rope once around the horizontal crossbeam. Then he laced the end of the rope through the loop where the rock was tied and pulled the rope tight around the crossbeam. Keeping a strong grasp on the rope, he wrapped his legs around it and inched down the rope to the ground. Once down, he stepped back and let go of the rope. The rock dropped, its weight pulling the rope off the crossbeam. Kaden coiled the rope, then hid it and the rock in some nearby bushes.

Emmett started the truck as Kaden hopped in and glanced at the clock on the dashboard. It wasn't even four yet. He wasn't late.

"I'm down, but what's up?" Kaden asked. He tried to sound like nothing was on his mind, but his heart was racing; he expected to hear Emmett say your dad's home.

But Emmett didn't say that. All he said was Gram sent me. Kaden suspected it meant the same thing. Neither of them said another word until they got halfway down the dirt road.

"Stop," Kaden said suddenly. They had just passed the muddy spot where a seep spring always kept a patch of road wet.

"Why?" Emmett asked. "You gotta take a leak?"

Kaden didn't answer. He jumped out of the truck, found a long stick, and stuck it upright in the center of the road where four sets of tire tracks indented the mud.

"What's that for?" Emmett asked as Kaden got back in the truck.

Kaden ignored him. If Emmett wasn't going to talk about what was going on, then he wasn't going to talk either. When they reached the main road, he expected Emmett to turn right, but instead, Emmett turned toward Promise.

"Where are we going?" Kaden asked.

"To the Purple Cow," Emmett answered. "I thought we'd get an ice cream."

"Now?" Kaden looked at Emmett. Emmett kept his eyes on the road. The strained silence said more than words. But when they pulled up to the diner with a life-size purple cow standing by the door, Kaden couldn't hold back anymore.

"I already know," he said.

"Already know what?" Emmett asked, the truck still running.

"About Dad."

"You do? But Gram asked me . . ." Emmett sounded confused. "How do you know?"

"I read part of the letter that came last Monday," Kaden

confessed. "And I saw him."

"You saw him?" Emmett repeated. He turned off the truck but neither of them opened a door.

"At the fire tower. He came there this afternoon. I saw him but he didn't see me. And I wasn't sure it was really him until you came. Then it was obvious."

"Obvious?" Emmett asked.

"You're usually a motormouth," Kaden explained, "but today you only said three words."

"Three words?" Emmett repeated.

"Three words. 'Gram sent me.' I knew right then."

"Well, I'll be." Emmett seemed genuinely surprised. "I guess we might as well go on in, then." He opened his truck door but Kaden didn't budge.

"I don't want to talk about Dad in there." Kaden nodded toward the Purple Cow.

"No way," Emmett said. "You might as well put your business on the six o'clock news if you even whisper a word in there."

"Then why did we come here? Shouldn't we be going home?"

"I'm supposed to keep you busy," Emmett said. "Your dad is at the cabins."

"Right now?" It was Kaden's turn to be surprised. *Dad*

must have turned around and gone back up the hill, he thought.

"Yeah, he's there now," Emmett answered. "Gram was afraid you'd come back and she wanted to have a chance to talk with your dad first. So she called me and asked me to—"

"She called you?" Kaden interrupted.

"Oops." Emmett looked sheepish. "Well, now I've gone and let the cat out of the bag. When Gram got the letter, I made her get a cell phone the next day. She put up a good fight but I won out in the end. She made me promise not to tell you, though, so don't you go and squeal on me."

"Okay," Kaden said.

"Now that you know she's got one, you ought to know the number, too. Just in case."

"Yeah, just in case," Kaden repeated. He guessed nobody was quite sure about Dad. Not himself, not Emmett, not even Gram.

"The number is 555-862-2165," Emmett said. "I picked out the easiest number for her. First, all those fives. Then eight equals six plus two, and then, times two equals sixteen and then there is one more five."

Kaden laughed. "I bet they really loved you in school."

"Actually, I had a lot of teachers baffled." Emmett grinned. "Don't know why; but let's go get some ice cream."

"Okay, but first I want to know—"

Emmett interrupted him. "I'm not supposed to tell you anything. I'm just suppose to keep you busy."

"But what's he like?" Kaden asked. "Will I like him?" He also wondered if his dad would like him, but he didn't say that out loud.

"That will be up to you to figure out," Emmett said.

CHAPTER FOUR

SALT AND PEPPER

Kaden and Emmett walked past the purple cow. A white board hung from its neck with the daily special written on it in purple marker. As they opened the door, the sound of a cow mooing announced their entry.

Inside, the walls were covered with photos of fiberglass cows. There was a Cow-boy with a Stetson hat, a bandana around its neck and spurs on its hooves. There was a Moss-Cow, a Cow-ch Potato, and a Cow-culator. Emmett slid into a booth by a Cow-lendar, a bright yellow Cow-ard, and a Cow-lifornia Cow on a beach towel wearing big sunglasses and a yellow polka-dot bikini. Kaden sat across from him, looking toward a mural of the inside of a dairy barn with three cows, their backsides facing into the restaurant. As part of the decorations, a real pitchfork leaned against the wall in the corner next to the mural's painted haystack.

It was before the dinner stampede, as Pillie called it, and they were the only ones in the restaurant. Elana pushed open the swinging door from the kitchen. She was the most popular girl in Kaden's class, but except at Pillie's, Kaden rarely spoke to her. At school, Kaden tried to stay clear of Elana, because wherever she was, Luke was always close by.

"Hi, Kaden. Hi, Emmett. What can I get you guys?" Elana said.

"Three Jumbo Lightning Moo-Creams," Emmett said.

"Three?" Kaden and Elana both said at the same time.

"Of course," Emmett said. "One for me, one for Kaden, and you'll need one, too."

"Me?" Elana said at the same time as Kaden said, "Elana?"

"Certainly. We don't want to eat in front of the young lady."

"I'm supposed to be helping," Elana said.

"You will be," Emmett replied. "Helping yourself to a delicious sundae."

"I mean . . . ," Elana started to explain.

"Oh, don't worry, your mom won't mind." Then in a loud voice Emmett yelled out, "Hey, Pillie, you mind if your daughter joins us for a sundae?"

Pillie came out of the kitchen. "No, I don't care, as long as she gets the salt and pepper shakers filled before the stampede. What are you having?"

"Jumbo Lightning Moo-Creams," Elana reported.

"Coming right up," Pillie said.

Elana followed her mom into the kitchen.

"Why are you getting Elana one?" Kaden asked. But before Emmett could answer, Elana returned holding large canisters of salt and pepper. Emmett kicked Kaden under the table.

"Ouch," Kaden said. "Why'd you kick me?"

"Go help her," Emmett whispered, giving his head a jerk toward Elana.

Kaden rolled his eyes at Emmett but slid out of the booth.

"Want some help?" he asked. He could feel his face turning red.

"Sure," Elana said. "Salt goes in the cows. They have four holes in their heads. Pepper in the bulls. They have horns and only two holes. Don't get them mixed up. Mom got really annoyed when Luke helped me."

Kaden had heard about Luke's pranks. Showing off to Elana, they had been going on for weeks. At first, it was just minor stuff like putting salt and pepper in the wrong shakers.

But then Pillie caught Luke red-handed leaving a dried-up cow patty on the floor under one of the mural's cows. She grabbed the pitchfork from the corner and chased Luke from the restaurant.

Mr. Woodhead, Luke's father, threatened to file assault charges against Pillie, but Sheriff O'Connor didn't want to be on Pillie's bad side. The Purple Cow was the only place in town to get a good cup of coffee. The sheriff made Luke clean up the cow manure and Pillie banned Luke from her restaurant.

Now as Kaden picked up a bull and poured in pepper, Pillie brought out three enormous sundaes. She put two purple flashlights on the table and headed back to the kitchen.

Kaden started to slide into the booth but Emmett stopped him. "Ladies first, Kaden."

Kaden stepped aside and let Elana slide in.

"What are these for?" Kaden asked, picking up one of the flashlights.

"You get one every time you order a Jumbo Lightning Moo-Cream," Elana said. "Mom read that cows' horns sometimes glow during a lightning storm. They're supposed to represent the lightning."

Without saying another word, the three of them dug into their ice cream, as a clock that looked like a cow ticked off the seconds, its tail twitching back and forth. Soon their spoons were scraping the last bites from the dishes.

"Moo-chas gracias, Emmett," Elana said as they slid from their seats. "See you Monday at school, Kaden."

"Yeah, see ya," Kaden answered.

When they left the restaurant, Kaden turned to Emmett. "Why did you invite Elana to have ice cream with us?"

"I thought it would be a good distraction," Emmett said, grinning. "Worked, didn't it?"

CHAPTER FIVE

NOT READY

As soon as Emmett started up the truck, all distractions made by Elana, ice cream sundaes, cows, and flashlights disappeared.

The closer they got to the cabins, the more nervous Kaden became. His heart was beating so hard when they pulled in the circle drive, he was certain Emmett could hear it over the sound of the truck's motor. The white pickup sat in front of Cabin Five. The cabin's door stood open. A fan gently ruffled the curtains in its opened window, but there was not a breath of wind outside, and Kaden felt like he couldn't breathe either.

Emmett pulled up in front of Gram's cabin, put the truck in park, but left it running.

"Aren't you coming in?" Kaden asked. He felt like he was going to be sick, all that ice cream on an empty and now nervous stomach.

"No, I don't think so, *mooo-cho* things to do at home," Emmett said, trying to lighten the tension. But when he looked at Kaden's face, Emmett reached down and turned the key. The truck became silent.

Kaden sat there. He felt paralyzed. He didn't think he could even open the door.

"Come on," Emmett said. "Let's get it over with."

Kaden got out of the truck. Emmett put his hand on his shoulder as they climbed the porch steps. There was no sound except the steady hum of Gram's fan coming through the screen door. Kaden opened the door and he and Emmett stepped inside.

Gram was sitting in the easy chair doing nothing. Just sitting. All alone. She stood up and put her hands on her hips.

"Where have you two been?" she asked gruffly, but before anyone could answer, she turned to Kaden. "Go to your cabin and wash up for dinner. I need to talk to Emmett."

"But—" Kaden started to ask where his dad was when Emmett interrupted him.

"Do what your Gram says."

Kaden started to protest again, but Emmett gave him

a barely perceptible shake of his head. Kaden usually paid attention to Emmett's subtle hints to keep quiet. This time, however, he ignored him and turned back to Gram.

"No," he said defiantly. "I'm staying right here."

"I'm only going to say it one more time. Go to your cabin."

Kaden stared straight into Gram's eyes. He was tired of being left in the dark.

"No. He's my father and I want to know what's going on."

Gram looked surprised. She stared at Kaden but when she crossed her arms in front of her, she turned on Emmett. "I told you not to tell," she said.

"He didn't," Kaden said. "I already knew. I saw him today at the tower."

Now Gram was really perplexed. "You saw him?"

"Yes, and I'm not going to my room. I'm going to go see my dad. I know he's in Cabin Five. What'd you do, tell him he had to go to his room, too?"

Suddenly the sound of a motor starting up came through the screen door. Kaden pushed past Emmett and darted out onto the porch just in time to see the white pickup spin its tires in the gravel as it turned onto the road toward town.

"Wait!" Kaden yelled, and ran after the truck. But the truck went around the bend before Kaden even got halfway down the circle drive.

Kaden stood, his hands balled into fists. He heard footsteps come up behind him. Gram put a hand on his shoulder, but Kaden jerked away and turned to face her.

"I had a right to see him! He's my father!" Kaden exploded. "And I would have if it weren't for you." Tears of anger rolled down his cheeks.

"And you, too!" he yelled at Emmett. "You both treat me like I'm a baby. Always saying, 'Go to your cabin, Kaden. Let's get ice cream, Kaden.' You're always talking about everything except what's on everyone's mind. You don't have to shelter me. I'm old enough to hear what's going on. So, what else are you keeping a secret from me? Did you tell Dad to leave? Did you make him promise to stay away?"

Kaden had almost worn out his anger but when Gram said nothing, it rekindled.

"Are you going to answer me for once?" he said harshly, spitting out each word. "Why did he leave?"

Gram still said nothing. Even Emmett looked at her, waiting to hear her answer. But Gram just stared past Kaden and Emmett, looking down the empty road, almost as if she were looking for a different scene, the way a life could have been. After a few seconds, she turned and looked directly at Kaden.

"I'm sorry," Gram said in the quietest and most sorrowful

voice Kaden had ever heard her use. "I tried to talk some sense into him, but he's not ready."

"What do you mean, not ready?" Kaden asked, still angry.

Gram looked straight at Kaden and said, "Your father is not ready to see you."

Monday, August 29

CHAPTER SIX

THE EXIT PLAN

It was the first day of school. The sky was just turning pink when the school bus pulled into the circle drive and stopped in front of Gram's cabin. It had been an uncomfortable weekend. Neither Gram nor Kaden had said a word about his dad or Friday's argument. Necessary conversations were brief and overly polite. Otherwise they kept their thoughts to themselves.

The anger had left Kaden but a sense of disappointment and puzzlement replaced it. All weekend, Gram's words echoed through his head. *Your father is not ready to see you.* Kaden had worried about seeing his dad yet never once thought his dad might be afraid of seeing him.

Something else about Gram's words kept nagging at him, too, and he worried that he might have misinterpreted his grandmother. Gram used that expression "you're not ready" quite a bit, and it always meant something different. Sometimes it meant he wasn't old enough. Other times, Gram used the same words when discussing Kaden's attitude, meaning Kaden needed to clean up his act. Gram also used those words to mean Kaden wasn't being responsible. Kaden kept bouncing back and forth, trying to interpret what Gram meant this time. *Was his dad afraid to see him, or did Gram decide Dad didn't have the right attitude or wasn't responsible enough?*

These questions had driven him crazy over the weekend, so now Kaden was actually glad it was finally Monday, his first day of middle school. He needed to think about something besides his dad. Kaden stepped up into the bus. Doris sat behind the wheel.

"Don't you look spiffy for the first day of school," Doris said. "Must have given up some of your hard-earned bucks in Chapston City."

"Yeah, Emmett took me," Kaden said. He thought about the quiet ride to Chapston City to buy school supplies. Kaden knew Emmett wouldn't explain Gram's words. So he just looked out the window, keeping his eyes peeled for a white pickup with a cargo carrier in the back. But the only white pickup he recognized had a magnetic sign stuck on the door with the eagle head emblem and the words UNITED STATES POSTAL SERVICE written in dark blue.

Now Kaden plopped down in the seat right behind Doris, feeling conspicuously new. New jeans, new sneakers, new T-shirt, even new socks and underwear. Just like the first day every year, Gram had insisted, but Kaden knew he was a sitting target for Luke.

"Don't take off yet," he told Doris. "Gram's coming today."

"Good," Doris replied. "It's been a long summer. Lots to catch up on."

Kaden was always the first on the bus and the last off. The bus always arrived a half hour earlier than it needed to because Doris enjoyed a cup of coffee with Emmett every morning before going on down the mountain into town. Kaden didn't mind. Unlike Gram, Emmett loved to bake.

"Not cook, mind you," he would say. "Bake."

Kaden could always count on something good in the morning. Cheese biscuits, apple crisp, or his favorite, homemade cinnamon rolls. Emmett's treats made a nice dessert to the bowl of lumpy oatmeal with raisins Gram placed in front of Kaden every morning.

Gram also liked "a little something," as she called it, and

even though she wouldn't admit it, she also enjoyed a bit of gossip with Doris. Gram didn't go every day but rode the bus to Emmett's at least a couple of times a week.

"I forgot," Doris said to Kaden as Gram climbed aboard, "you'll get first choice of middle-school seats now, won't you?"

"Yep," Kaden answered, "and I'm taking this one, right here."

Promise Elementary and Promise Middle School were both squished into the same building. A crow flying over would see its hallways made a big rectangle with a courtyard in the middle. The left hallway held middle-school class-rooms. Elementary classrooms were on the right. A back hallway completed the rectangle leading to an all-purpose room that served as both cafeteria and gym. Opposite the all-purpose room was the library, with a set of glass doors that opened into the courtyard.

A one-way drive for buses only went down the left side of the school, across the back and then up the right side. A cars-only drive curved past the front. Beyond that was a wide strip of grass and then the school parking lot. Standing prominently in the grass were a flagpole and a sign saying PROMISE ELEMENTARY AND MIDDLE SCHOOL.

Only teachers and car riders entered through the front

doors. All other students entered and exited in back. Doris required middle-school students to sit at the front of her bus in the morning because they would get off first. In the afternoon, when the middle schoolers loaded first, she had them sit at the back. She was very proud of her entry and exit system and boasted she could load and unload a bunch of kids faster and with fewer problems than anybody in Hill County.

Kaden figured the seat right behind Doris would be the best one. He could be down the steps and out the bus door before anyone could push, shove, elbow, or trip him.

The bus pulled out from the McCrorys' cabins, went around the bend, down the hill, and pulled into Emmett's driveway. With the bus windows down in the late August heat, Kaden could smell cinnamon rolls before Doris even opened the door.

Doris and Gram walked through the kitchen and into the dining room, taking their usual spots at the dining room table. Kaden stayed with Emmett in the kitchen. While Emmett poured coffee and put cinnamon rolls on a platter, Kaden poured himself a glass of milk.

"Any new pictures on the wall?" Kaden asked, even though he knew the answer.

"No, none since your birthday last month," Emmett

stated.

They were referring to the wall at the far end of the kitchen, where four large cork bulletin boards hung. Each bulletin board was loaded with photographs. Layers upon unorganized layers overlapping each other, depicting years and years. There were babies, kids, people holding fish they'd caught, trophies they'd won. Dogs and horses, kittens and puppies. Sunsets, flowers, and snowy landscapes. The collection had long ago outgrown the bulletin boards and covered the entire wall. It was now creeping over the doorframe and wending itself around the corner. It reminded Kaden of ivy covering a medieval castle, a living wall. But this one was made of a lifetime of memories, and Emmett could tell you the story living behind each picture. Kaden was so familiar with the stories, they had become his stories, too, even though many occurred before he was born and were about people he'd never met.

"There's your birthday picture." Emmett pointed to Kaden holding a big piece of poster board with a gigantic number eleven written on it. There were eight other similar pictures scattered here and there, one for each year since he turned three. Emmett took the cinnamon rolls into the dining room, but Kaden stayed, looking at the wall. There were several pictures of his dad but there wasn't one in which his father was over fourteen years old.

Kaden looked closely at one of the pictures, trying to see if there was any resemblance between the young teen and the grown man with the white truck. But he hadn't gotten a good look at the man. Not enough to compare with a twenty-year-old photograph.

Back on the bus, Kaden put his backpack on the seat to guarantee nobody would sit next to him. He didn't think anyone would, but just as a precaution. Entering town, the bus wound through neighborhoods and quickly filled with students. The last house was Luke's. No one had taken the seat behind Kaden but now Luke plopped down in it. Kaden pretended to be very interested in looking out the window.

"I bet he held up a store for those new clothes." Luke's voice was clearly heard over the din of voices. Several giggles followed.

"Should have nabbed a new backpack while he was at it," Luke continued. "He's used the same backpack for years."

Kaden kept quiet and continued to stare out the window, pretending he didn't hear. Luke was right, though. It was the same backpack he'd had since third grade. Gram had patched up holes and countlessly sewn the shoulder straps back on, but each fall she said it would last another year.

The bus came to a stop and Kaden sprang from his seat. He entered the building, thinking Doris wasn't the only one with a superb exit plan.

CHAPTER SEVEN

A-TEAM

At Promise Middle School there was no surprise about which students would be in Kaden's classes. The same eighteen students all started kindergarten together and would be together until they graduated from eighth grade. Then they would go to Hill County Regional High School, which combined students from Promise, Thredt, and several other small towns in the area.

Likewise, there would be no surprise about who his teachers would be. Every year, the same three teachers shared sixth, seventh, and eighth grades. Mr. Herd always taught math and science. Mr. Clary taught reading and English, and Ms. Ales taught a class of history to each middle-school grade, then spent the rest of the day as the librarian for both elementary and middle school. The art, music, and PE teachers also taught both elementary and middle-school classes.

Entering the school, most of the kids turned down the back hallway toward the cafeteria. Some would eat breakfast, others just hung out for the seventeen minutes until first bell. But Kaden hurried straight ahead to Ms. Ales's room. Much to his surprise, there was a kid already in there. Kaden had never seen him before and he was sitting at Kaden's desk. Every year his classroom had four rows of desks, with five desks in each. Kaden always sat at the same desk. The desk in the back corner by the window. And ever since first grade, no kids ever sat in the desk next to his or in front of it.

Kaden liked being isolated in the back corner and wasn't happy a new kid was taking his spot. Someone like Luke would just walk up and demand that the new kid move. But Kaden didn't like confrontation. Without looking at the kid, Kaden walked across the room and dumped his backpack on the desk in front of him.

"Hi," the boy said cheerfully.

"Hi," Kaden replied unenthusiastically. He slid into the seat and busied himself with opening his backpack. He didn't say another word and was glad the new kid didn't either.

First bell rang. Other students came into the room in groups and clusters, all laughing and talking with each other. They immediately noticed the new kid but no one spoke to him. Nobody chose the seat next to him either, but the whispering started almost instantly. Kaden saw Luke say something to Elana behind his hand. Elana looked back toward Kaden and the new boy. The new boy waved at Elana and she turned quickly back around. Luke said something else and laughed. Others around him laughed, too, but Elana gave only a halfhearted smile.

Ms. Ales came into the room talking with a woman. Kaden had never seen her before either. Several students whispered, "Who's that?"

When second bell rang, Ms. Ales picked up a small brass bell on her desk and rang it. Everyone had heard Ms. Ales's little bell in library since kindergarten and all knew to quiet down.

"Welcome to middle school, A-Team," Ms. Ales said to the class. She used the same nickname with every class, every year. "I hope you all had a great summer. You should have your schedules. They were mailed to you along with the middle-school handbook. Some of the rules are different from elementary, so I suggest you read it. Now I want to introduce a couple people. I'm sure you noticed we have a new student."

The new kid gave a big grin and a little wave. Then leaning across his desk, he whispered over Kaden's shoulder, "Here it comes."

Kaden had no idea what he was talking about.

"Our new student's name is Yo-Yo Strokowski," Ms. Ales stated, as if there were nothing at all unusual about his name.

"Yo-Yo? You gotta be kidding!" Luke called out. Most of the class giggled. Kaden sat there, glad the negative attention was on someone else for a change.

"A-Team!" Ms. Ales said sternly. "We will have none of that. Yes, he has an unusual name." Ms. Ales looked at Yo-Yo, gave a big smile, and continued. "Welcome to our school, Yo-Yo. I'm sure you'll make a wonderful addition to the A-Team."

Yo-Yo grinned at Ms. Ales, then leaned forward again and whispered to Kaden, "That wasn't too bad. I've had it worse. Sometimes even the teacher laughs or has a smart comment. Believe me, I've heard them all."

Ms. Ales turned back to the class. "We also have a new teacher. This is Mrs. Strokowski, Yo-Yo's mom. She's the new music teacher."

Mrs. Strokowski stepped forward. "I'm glad to meet the A-Team," she said. Kaden wondered how long it would take her to realize Ms. Ales had nine A-Teams, one for each grade.

"I look forward to having you in music class every Tuesday. And if you decide to join band, you'll be with me after lunch on Tuesday and Thursday, too, instead of study hall."

"Next comes the explanation," Yo-Yo whispered.

"I'm sure you noticed my son has an unusual name. He shares it with one of the most talented musicians of our time, Yo-Yo Ma. Has anyone ever heard of Yo-Yo Ma?"

No one raised their hand. Mrs. Strokowski stared toward her son, and he unenthusiastically raised his hand to shoulder height.

When his mom's attention turned back toward the rest of the class, Yo-Yo leaned forward and whispered again. "Now for the assignment," he said.

"Well, that will be our first assignment, then," Mrs. Strokowski stated. "Tomorrow, when you come to music, I want you to know what instrument Yo-Yo Ma plays. But this won't be hard. It just so happens he's playing tonight on public television at seven o'clock."

"That leaves Kaden out. His family doesn't have a TV," Luke blurted.

"Really?" Yo-Yo asked Kaden.

Kaden slouched down in his seat, wishing he could become invisible behind the backpack on his desk.

"Maybe his dad can steal one for him," Luke said.

"That's enough, Luke!" Ms. Ales snapped. She turned to Mrs. Strokowski, and in a nicer voice said, "I'm sure Kaden will come up with the answer without a television."

After first period, Kaden stopped briefly at his locker. When he entered Mr. Herd's science classroom, the new kid was already sitting in the back corner. As much as Kaden hurried after each bell, Yo-Yo beat him to the back corner seat all morning. Kaden ignored the comments the short boy with dark hair and blue eyes constantly whispered to him from behind. At lunch, however, Kaden was surprised to see that his corner spot in the cafeteria remained empty. Yo-Yo was in the middle of the cafeteria, surrounded by Luke, Elana, and several others.

I was wondering how long it would take Luke to recruit the new kid, Kaden thought. But, after lunch, Yo-Yo was back in the corner in what was becoming Yo-Yo's seat, and Kaden had no option but to sit in front of the new boy.

CHAPTER EIGHT

THE STOWAWAY

At the end of seventh period, Kaden was ready for part two of his "first off, last on" bus plan. When the bell rang, everyone raced to the buses but Kaden took his time. He hung back until everyone boarded. Then he sat alone in the first seat dedicated to middle schoolers, staying away from the back seats where Luke was.

Doris pulled forward to the other doors. Yo-Yo was mixed in with the waiting elementary students. He handed Doris a note. She read it and nodded.

"Elementary kids sit in the front half in the afternoon," she said to him, closing the door.

"I'm not in elementary, I'm just short," Yo-Yo said.

"I'm actually a sixth grader."

"Looks more like a fourth grader," Luke called out from the back of the bus. "You better keep him up front with the babies, Doris."

Doris ignored Luke. "Well, go sit in back, then," she said to Yo-Yo. "You're holding up my schedule."

Yo-Yo walked down the aisle, looking back and forth at each seat as he went. When he got to Kaden's seat, he stopped, picked up Kaden's backpack, and sat down, putting Kaden's backpack on his own lap.

"I was hoping I stowed away on the right bus," he said to Kaden. "I know there's only two, but it was a fifty-fifty chance getting the right one. I was afraid it would leave without me, but it wouldn't matter. It's not like I'm riding the bus home. I'm a walker. My house is the red one two doors down from the school."

"If you're supposed to be a walker, how did you get permission to ride the bus?" Kaden cut in when Yo-Yo paused for a breath.

"I had my mom write a note. She's not ready to go home yet, but the bus will be back to school about the time she is," Yo-Yo said. "She's a walker, too. It's not much farther walking home than walking to the parking lot, so she's not going to bother driving. But she won't let me go home alone. She says she needs my help to carry stuff but I know that's just an excuse. She treats me like I'm a baby 'cause I'm small for my age, but I'm working on that. . . ."

Kaden didn't think Yo-Yo would ever stop talking, and obviously, nobody else did either. The whole bus was quiet, listening. Luke finally interrupted him.

"Working on what, getting taller?" he jeered.

"No, I like being compact." Yo-Yo looked down the aisle to answer. "I've noticed some of those tall guys get left with no muscle." The entire back of the bus laughed. Luke was the tallest boy in sixth grade and almost as tall as the tallest eighth grader. But he was also one of the skinniest. His arms looked like they had no muscle at all. Just skin and bones.

Kaden was surprised Yo-Yo spoke up to Luke like that. *This Yo-Yo kid must not have been recruited after all*, he thought.

Doris pulled up in front of Luke's house. When Luke walked up the aisle, he grabbed Kaden's backpack from Yo-Yo's lap. Kaden heard the shoulder strap rip as Luke slid it down the aisle like a bowling ball. It crashed into the front of the bus next to Doris.

"This is your first and only warning, Luke Woodhead," Doris said. "Any more behavior like that, and you'll be kicked off my bus. You shouldn't even be a bus rider.

You live close enough to walk."

"You know my dad won't stand for that," Luke said.

"Just because your dad's on the school board doesn't mean I'm going to allow misbehavior on my bus and I'm sure the rest of the school board would back me."

Yo-Yo went to the front of the bus after Luke got off.

"Sorry," Yo-Yo apologized to Doris, picking up Kaden's backpack. "It was my fault. I egged him on."

"No, Luke's behavior is Luke's choice," Doris told Yo-Yo. "But it is your fault you're holding up my schedule again. My bus doesn't move while students are standing." She sounded gruff but gave Yo-Yo a big smile.

Yo-Yo trotted down the aisle with Kaden's backpack banging into his knees and handed it to him.

"Sorry, the strap ripped when he grabbed it," he said.

"That's okay, it's been fixed a gazillion times. But you'd better watch out. Luke's not someone you should mess around with."

"Not at all worried," Yo-Yo said. "I'm a Navy brat and I've been to a bunch of schools. There's always a Luke around. I had him figured out by lunchtime. Like I said, I had a fifty-fifty chance of getting on Luke's bus. I always like to let bullies know right away that I'm not afraid of them, even though I usually am. You've probably noticed, I'm not exactly the biggest kid around. But buses are great places. Lots of witnesses."

"Does your mom know you wanted to ride the bus just to make your stand with Luke?"

"Heck no," Yo-Yo said. "She wouldn't let me out of her sight if she thought I was going up against someone like him. I told her I wanted to ride around to see where all my new friends live. Which really isn't a lie."

Yo-Yo was looking out the window. The bus had let the last town kid off and was now halfway up the mountain.

"Everyone said you live a long way out of town. I can't believe this is in the same district. So all the rumors are true, aren't they."

Kaden tensed up when he heard the word "rumors." The word always led to his father and he wasn't willing to talk about that.

"Mostly," he said, but quickly changed the subject. "Where'd you live before you came here?" Kaden figured he could avoid the topic of his father if he could keep Yo-Yo talking. That obviously wasn't difficult. The kid never shut up.

"I've lived in fourteen different states, that's more than one per year, but ever since kindergarten, we managed to stay in the same place for a whole school year so Mom can teach. Promise is the seventh school I've been to.

The last place I lived . . ."

Yo-Yo kept talking but Kaden had stopped listening. They were driving past the dirt road leading to the fire tower. Kaden glanced up it. A white pickup truck was moving toward the main road. Kaden scrambled over Yo-Yo and ran to the back of the bus. He reached the back windows just in time to see the white truck turn onto the main road. But it didn't turn toward the cabins. The truck turned left.

Angrily, Kaden slammed his hand down on the back of the seat.

"What's the matter?" Yo-Yo said. He was sitting on his knees, looking over the back of the seat at Kaden. Kaden said nothing. The bus pulled into the circle drive.

"So the rumors are true!" Yo-Yo exclaimed. "You do live in cabins, don't you? This is really awesome! Living way up here in the woods. How sweet is this? Can I get off with you? I'll call my mom and have her pick me up. She won't care. I can't believe this. I've never had a friend who lived in the wilderness before!"

Yo-Yo was already heading down the aisle, talking excitedly all the way. But when Kaden saw his dad's truck turn toward town, it brought back all the anger from the previous Friday, and Yo-Yo's incessant gibbering just added fuel to the fire. Kaden grabbed his backpack by the broken strap and pushed past Yo-Yo.

"Would you shut up," Kaden said angrily. "You're not getting off the bus with me. I don't need a friend."

Yo-Yo was surprised at the sudden outburst. "I just thought—" he started, but Kaden interrupted him.

"Just. Shut. Up."

"Kaden!" Doris said as she pulled the lever to open the door. "What's wrong with you?"

"You too, Doris. Both of you. Just shut up and leave me alone!" Kaden yelled, and stomped from the bus.

Kaden stormed past Gram's and flung open his cabin door. Instantly, Gram's voice came over the intercom.

"What was all that yelling about?" Gram said.

"Nothing. I'm going for a walk," Kaden said, tossing his backpack on his bed.

"Not until you're ready to speak nicely to me, you're not," Gram said back. Kaden ignored her, and letting the screen door slam, walked away from the cabins.

CHAPTER NINE

SURPRISES

By the time Kaden reached the muddy spot in the road, he had calmed down. He knew he wasn't angry with the new kid. Yo-Yo had even called him a friend. He wasn't angry with Doris either. Or with Gram. He was angry with his father. His father, who wasn't ready to see him yet. His father, who was certain to have seen the bus go by and would have known Kaden would be coming home from school. His father, who had chosen to turn left, not right.

The stick was no longer standing upright in the middle of the muddy patch. One boot print was in the mud and the stick now lay near the edge of the road. Kaden put the stick back in the middle of the muddy patch. He started to walk on but came back. He found a small branch with several dead leaves still on it and laid it in the muddy patch. *If Dad comes up here again*, Kaden thought, *he'll have the stick all figured out. He may put it back next time to make it look like nobody's driven up the road.* But Kaden knew his father wouldn't pay any attention to the leaves. He'd drive right over them, crushing them in the mud.

Feeling satisfied, Kaden walked on to the tower. Kubla greeted him, cawing from the landing as Kaden took the rope from its hiding place in the bushes.

Kaden swung the rock back and forth, back and forth, letting out a little more rope with each swing. On the third swing, he let go. The rock, with its rope tail, went up, over the crossbeam and then back down, thudding on the ground. This time, he threaded the rock through a loop tied at the opposite end of the rope, then dropped the rock to the ground again. He pulled on the rope hand over hand until it tightened around the beam.

Tightly grasping the rope above his head, Kaden lifted his feet and twisted them around the rope. When he straightened his legs, he was dangling a foot above the ground. One hand at a time, he reached above his head and pulled himself a little higher. Twisting and straightening and pulling, he repeated this procedure over and over, looking like an inchworm creeping up the rope.

It wasn't until he balanced on his stomach over the metal beam twenty feet above the ground that Kaden saw a large plastic bag on the landing. It was stuffed with something big and bulky and tied shut with a twisty. Kubla stood on the bag. Wondering what was in it and who left it there, Kaden flung a leg over the beam and carefully scooted backward until he reached the landing. Kubla jumped to his shoulder. Kaden unwound the twisty, and together, the boy and the bird looked inside.

Kaden couldn't believe his eyes. Inside was a brand-new backpack. It still had tags on it. It wasn't an ordinary school backpack. It was a daypack a hunter might use, with a woodland camo pattern that would blend in perfectly with the fallen branches and leaf litter of the woods. It had all sorts of pockets, webbed straps, and tie-downs. On the side was a mesh pocket with a plastic canteen. Kaden opened each zipper compartment and looked inside. Empty. No notes. No cards. Not even a receipt.

Kubla put his head in and out of the opened pockets as if he, too, were looking for a clue to identify the mysterious gift giver. But Kaden knew it had to be from his father. Gram wouldn't buy him a new one. If Emmett did, he wouldn't fling it up on the landing.

"How did he know I needed a backpack?" Kaden asked Kubla. "Maybe he went into my room last Friday. Maybe he saw my old one sitting there. What do you think, Kubla?"

Kaden suddenly felt very lonely. Except for Luke and his followers, the kids at school were nice enough, but they generally just left him alone. He was never included in any activities outside the classroom, and over the years he had gotten more and more used to being a loner. Now he thought of the new kid who had called him a friend. The new kid who didn't mind sitting near him at school. Kaden let out a sigh. After his outburst on the bus, he doubted Yo-Yo would be sitting behind him anymore.

Kubla stopped tugging at a zipper pull and, cocking his head to one side, muttered to Kaden. Kaden gently ruffled the feathers on the bird's head.

"Don't worry," he said. "You're a great friend and nobody will ever take your place. But it'd be kind of nice to have a human friend to discuss things with, too." Kaden sighed and shook his head. "I guess I blew that chance, though, didn't I."

That night, Kaden pulled out the "M" encyclopedia. The first entry said the letter "M" was the thirteenth letter in the alphabet and probably came from a hieroglyphic sign to represent water. The second entry was "Ma, Yo-Yo."

"What are you looking up?" Gram said from the kitchen.

"I'm supposed to find out what instrument a guy named Yo-Yo Ma played," Kaden said.

"Plays," Gram corrected. "He's not dead and he plays a cello."

Kaden looked up with surprise.

"That's right," Gram said. "I do know a few things. And I always liked Yo-Yo Ma."

Kaden couldn't remember Gram ever playing any music. But there was an old turntable and a pile of records stuck in a corner in Cabin One, the junk cabin. They had been collecting dust for years.

Kaden read more from the encyclopedia. "Wow," he said. "He played for President Kennedy when he was only seven and now he plays a 250-year-old cello he named Petunia because some little girl asked if it had a name."

That night as Kaden lay in bed, through the intercom he heard Gram's front door squeak open. Then through the open window he heard Gram walk past his cabin to Cabin One and open its door. A few minutes later, Cabin One's door shut and Gram's footsteps could be heard walking back to Cabin Three. Over the intercom, Kaden heard sounds of things being moved around. Soon the low sweet notes of a cello drifted through the intercom into Kaden's room. Kaden listened and smiled. Gram hadn't done anything surprising like this for as long as he could remember.

Tuesday, August 30

CHAPTER TEN

ACCEPTED

Gram didn't notice the new backpack, or at least she didn't say anything about it. But Doris did. When Kaden apologized to her, she just said, "Apology accepted," then nodded toward the backpack and added, "I see Chapston City profited from Luke's behavior." Kaden didn't reply.

Luke noticed the backpack, too.

"Ooh, new backpack," he said sarcastically, sitting behind Kaden on the bus. "And camo, too. Gonna use it to hide stolen loot?"

Kaden ignored him but smiled to himself. He knew despite his sarcasm Luke was envious of the backpack. There wasn't a boy in school who wouldn't love to have a backpack like that one. But Luke would never say anything like "awesome backpack," especially to Kaden.

As Kaden quickly scrambled off the bus, he wondered what Yo-Yo would say. Even after yesterday, even if he blew having Yo-Yo as a friend, Kaden doubted the new boy would give him the silent treatment when he saw the new backpack. Kaden chuckled to himself. Actually, he doubted if Yo-Yo was even capable of being silent.

When Kaden entered Ms. Ales's room, he instantly noticed Yo-Yo's backpack on a desk in the middle of the room. Right behind Elana's desk, kitty-cornered to Luke's. Someone's history textbook sat on the desk behind Yo-Yo's, claiming that seat.

Kaden crossed the room and swung his backpack onto his usual desk. He knew what had happened. Luke had informed Yo-Yo who Kaden was, that he came from a bad family, had bad blood. Yo-Yo had also been out to the cabins and saw how differently he and Gram lived. Now it was obvious. Yo-Yo had teamed up with Luke and Elana. Kaden had hoped it would be like it was yesterday, that Yo-Yo would talk to him, that Yo-Yo thought of him as a friend. But the backpack across the room told him otherwise.

Once again, Kaden felt angry. Angry at himself this time. It was all his fault, he told himself. He was the one who had yelled at Yo-Yo. He was the one who said he didn't need a friend.

Kaden laid his head on his backpack and closed his eyes, dreading the first bell. Dreading seeing Yo-Yo prance into the room, laughing with Luke and Elana, laughing about Kaden, proving he didn't need Kaden as a friend.

"Hey," Yo-Yo's voice called out suddenly. Kaden startled. He hadn't heard Yo-Yo come in.

"I tried to hurry but Mom made me help carry boxes, so I couldn't be here to tell you when you first got here." Yo-Yo didn't sound angry. He sounded like nothing had even happened yesterday on the bus.

"Tell me what?" Kaden asked.

"We're moving," Yo-Yo announced.

"Moving? You just got here. Is your dad being stationed somewhere else already?"

"My family's not moving," Yo-Yo answered. "My dad retired. He's not in the Navy anymore. We're here to stay."

"But you said you were moving," Kaden said.

"Not me. Us. You and me. We're moving."

"Huh?" Kaden said.

"Nothing says 'loser' more than sitting in the back corner," Yo-Yo said.

"You sat in the back corner yesterday," Kaden said.

"I always grab the back corner on the first day at a new school. That way I can see the entire classroom. Check everyone out. See their reactions when my name is announced. You can tell a lot from reactions."

"Oh yeah? What did you learn from my reaction?"

"A lot. First off, you didn't laugh when you heard my name, or even smile, even though everyone else did. So, you're not the type to make fun of others. And second, you're your own man. You didn't follow along with the crowd, but . . ." Yo-Yo hesitated.

"But what?" Kaden said.

"I probably shouldn't say this after seeing how you can have a bit of a temper," Yo-Yo continued. "I don't know what that was all about on the bus yesterday, but it came to me on the way back home."

"What came to you?" Kaden said.

"That I was in your usual seat in every class yesterday and nobody ever sat in the desk beside me. So I made another deduction. You always sit back here by yourself. Nobody in front of you, nobody beside you." Yo-Yo paused, tilted his head, and looked at Kaden. "You're not very popular, are you?"

"Who says I want to be popular? Luke's popular. Who wants to be like him?"

"Luke's not popular; people just act like they like him.

They're afraid not to," Yo-Yo said.

"What's that got to do with moving?"

"You can't get friends sitting back in the corner by yourself. Before you know it . . ." Yo-Yo suddenly stopped talking, finally noticing what was on Kaden's desk. "Hey, wicked backpack!" he said. "Can I see?" He grabbed the backpack and looked through each compartment, all the time talking about how sweet it was and what each compartment could hold. Kaden expected Yo-Yo to ask where he got it, but after he'd gone through each pocket, Yo-Yo went back to the previous subject.

"So, there's our new seats, near Luke and Elana," Yo-Yo said, pointing toward the middle of the room.

"I don't think where I sit will change my popularity," Kaden said, but Yo-Yo ignored him. He took Kaden's backpack and crossed the room.

"Yours . . . ," Yo-Yo said, picking up the history book and plopping Kaden's backpack on the desk, "and mine." Yo-Yo put the history book down beside his own backpack.

First bell rang and voices started coming toward them. Before anyone entered the room, Kaden asked, "Why these seats?"

"It's all about location. It's easier to whisper over a shoulder than side to side. And, being more used to talking to others in class, I can get away with turning around to talk better than you can."

"But why so close to Luke?" Kaden asked.

"Being close to Luke shows you're not afraid of him. But you want to stay behind him so you can keep your eye on him. Make him have to turn around to see you. But not directly behind him where he can get to you easily."

"And Elana?"

"She's cute, you have to admit it." Yo-Yo grinned. "Besides, she's not bad if you get her away from Luke."

"Yeah, I guess," Kaden said, "but the only place where she's not around Luke is at Pillie's. Luke's banned from the Purple Cow, but you'll never get Elana away from Luke at school."

"Patience, Kaden, patience. You can't expect miracles overnight," Yo-Yo answered. "I've only been here one day."

Kaden laughed. It suddenly seemed like it had been a month since yesterday. And if someone asked Kaden what his impressions were of Yo-Yo, Kaden would have to say besides being a bit hyper, Yo-Yo was the easiest person in the world to make friends with.

Kaden and Yo-Yo sat down at their new locations as the other students piled into the classroom. Luke came in beside Elana, took one look at Kaden, and marched straight toward him. As he passed Yo-Yo, he reached out and shoved Yo-Yo's backpack and history book to the floor. Then he turned to Kaden.

"What are you sitting here for? Nobody said you could come out of solitary confinement," Luke sneered. He picked up the corner of Kaden's desk and tipped it over. "Get back to your corner and take that compact little punk with you."

The room quieted, waiting to see what would happen next. But before anything could happen between Kaden and Luke, Yo-Yo jumped up, grabbed Kaden's backpack from the floor, and leaped over the toppled desk onto a chair. A row of desks and an aisle separated him from Luke.

"Hey, everybody, isn't Kaden's backpack wicked?" Yo-Yo started saying, holding the backpack up over his head for all to see. Everyone's attention was instantly drawn away from Luke as Yo-Yo continued talking. "I don't know any kid who has a backpack like this one. And I can't believe where Kaden gets to live! I know you guys have known each other forever, and I'm just the new kid, but I heard all these rumors yesterday, so I sneaked onto the bus just to see if they were true, and like I said, I couldn't believe it! Kaden really does live in cabins out in the woods. Most people only get to go someplace like that when they go on vacation, but Kaden gets to live there every day and . . ."

Everyone seemed mesmerized by Yo-Yo, who was talking so fast, it was hard to actually know where one sentence stopped and another began. Nobody noticed that Ms. Ales had walked in and was ringing her little brass bell until Kaden pulled Yo-Yo down from the chair, clamped his hand over Yo-Yo's mouth, and loudly said, "Yo-Yo, shut up!"

The words were the same as the ones he yelled on the bus the day before, but this time, there was no anger in Kaden's voice. This time, he had a smile on his face. And, except for Luke, the rest of the class was laughing. Not at Kaden, but with him.

Saturday, September 3

CHAPTER ELEVEN

ALL FIGURED OUT

The rest of the week went as usual for a first week of school. Teachers got back into their routines and students got back into theirs. But talking and laughing with a friend was not at all Kaden's usual routine and he was enjoying every minute. For once, the school year seemed promising.

Each day that week, Kaden went to the fire tower, just to check, but there were no more surprises. The stick was still standing in the muddy spot. The leaves were not crushed by tires. No more gifts were found on the landing. Kaden was frustrated about not meeting his father yet, but he kept thinking about what Yo-Yo had said. Miracles didn't happen overnight. But every time he lifted the new backpack, he knew his father had thought of him and that seemed promising, too.

The first day of Labor Day weekend was wet and windy. After lunch, Kaden went to the junk cabin and took out all the old vinyl record albums. He brought them to Gram's cabin, cleared a space under the kitchen sink, and stacked them in there.

"Hand me that one," Gram said, looking over his shoulder. She put the album on the turntable and carefully moved the player's arm so the needle rested in the groove. A jazz trumpet solo came through the speakers.

Kaden went back to his cabin. Sitting at his desk, he listened to the music through the intercom as he worked on a model of a P-38. He was about to glue the fuselage together when through the intercom he heard a knock on Gram's front door. Kaden immediately thought of his father. He quickly climbed across his bed to look out the window. A big black SUV sat in front of Gram's cabin. Kaden went back to his desk to listen.

Over the intercom he was surprised to hear Mrs. Strokowski's voice. "Hello, are you Mrs. McCrory?"

"I may be," Gram answered. "What do you want?"

Kaden didn't wait to hear Mrs. Strokowski's answer. Mrs. Strokowski was nice and he didn't know what Gram might say. Kaden charged out of his cabin. He took the porch steps in one leap and landed behind Mrs. Strokowski.

"Gram, this is Mrs. Strokowski, my music teacher." Gram didn't move.

"Who's that in the car?" she said, looking beyond Mrs. Strokowski.

Kaden turned around. Yo-Yo had his nose jammed up against the rain-streaked window.

"That's Yo-Yo," Kaden said.

Mrs. Strokowski started to explain his name, just like she did with the class, but Gram cut her off. "I got that all figured out," she said. "What I haven't got figured out is what you want."

Kaden pushed past Mrs. Strokowski and opened the screen door.

"Come on in," he said.

Gram gave him an irritated look but stepped aside to let Mrs. Strokowski enter.

"Better get your friend and go to your cabin while I talk with your teacher," Gram said, turning off the record player.

Kaden jumped from the porch, motioning for Yo-Yo to follow him.

"Where are we going?" Yo-Yo called out, dodging puddles.

"My cabin."

Yo-Yo followed Kaden in and looked around. Bent deer hooves over the bed held a BB gun, and a fish was mounted on the wall over his desk.

"Wicked!" Yo-Yo exclaimed. "You didn't tell me you have a whole cabin to yourself."

Kaden turned and put his index finger to his mouth.

"Shh," he whispered, "I want to hear what they're saying. And they can hear everything we say, too."

"I came because you haven't signed Kaden up for band," Mrs. Strokowski's voice came over the intercom. She sounded nervous and was talking real fast. Kaden knew Gram would just stare at her, letting her ramble and ramble, but nothing Mrs. Strokowski said would make any difference. Only Emmett could sway Gram to change her mind.

"Don't you want Kaden to play an instrument? Be part of the band? He might go on to play in the jazz band in high school. You were playing jazz. Maybe Kaden would be interested in jazz. The kids have a lot of fun. Both the marching band and the jazz band get to take a lot of field trips and—"

"Oh no," Kaden blurted out. Mrs. Strokowski stopped talking.

"Kaden, don't eavesdrop," Gram said. Then the red light on one of the intercoms in Kaden's room turned black.

"Well, that's the end of that," Kaden whispered to Yo-Yo.

"Your mom just gave playing in band the kiss of death."

"What do you mean?" Yo-Yo whispered back.

Before Kaden answered him, he grabbed his pillow and smothered the intercoms.

"Gram doesn't believe in fun or field trips." He had stopped whispering but kept his voice very quiet.

"What's with the pillow?" Yo-Yo asked.

"Gram can turn off her intercom anytime she wants so I can't hear her, but if I turn mine off so she can't hear me, the little red light on her intercom will go out."

"So," Yo-Yo said.

"Then she'd know I turned off my intercom," Kaden explained. "I tried it once and for two weeks, I had to go back to living in her cabin. But my pillow muffles our voices, and if we're quiet, she can't hear us."

"Doesn't that bother you, having her listening all the time?"

"I usually don't have anybody here to talk to."

"What about when you're on the phone?"

"We don't have a phone." Kaden knew Gram secretly owned one but he wasn't going to tell Yo-Yo that.

"I didn't used to but I finally convinced my mom to get me a cell phone in case of emergencies," Yo-Yo said. "My number is 555-862-9696, if you want to call me. The first four numbers don't mean anything, but the six and two spells out Ma, and the rest spells out Yo-Yo. Isn't that cool? I picked it out myself."

"I'm not talking about a cell phone," Kaden said, thinking Yo-Yo sounded a lot like Emmett. "We don't have any phone. We have to use Emmett's."

"Who's Emmett?"

"Our neighbor. He lives down the road in the house with all the signs."

Suddenly a muffled voice came from under the pillow. Kaden quickly picked up the pillow. Both red lights were shining again.

"Kaden, did you hear me?" Gram said. "Yo-Yo's mom is waiting for him."

Kaden and Yo-Yo hurried to Gram's cabin. Mrs. Strokowski was on the porch asking Gram to think it over during the weekend when Emmett's pickup pulled in. He came every Saturday afternoon to get Gram's grocery list, and Kaden almost always went with him to the Big Apple.

"Are you a promise or a threat?" Emmett said to Yo-Yo as he joined the group on the porch.

Yo-Yo obviously didn't know Thredt was the town on the other side of Promise and was Promise Middle School's biggest rival. He also didn't know Emmett asked that question of just about every kid he saw.

"I'm not sure," Yo-Yo said, glancing questioningly at Kaden. "I'm Yo-Yo."

Emmett laughed. "I've never had a kid admit he's a yo-yo before. Are you moody or bouncy?"

"He didn't say he was a yo-yo," Kaden told Emmett. "He said he is Yo-Yo. That's his name. And this is his mom, Mrs. Strokowski. She's the new music teacher."

"I stand corrected," Emmett said to Yo-Yo, then turned to Mrs. Strokowski. "Good afternoon, ma'am. I'm Emmett Adams. If you decide to start up a town choir, I'll sing in it."

"Is that a promise or a threat?" Yo-Yo quickly said, giving Emmett his best grin.

"Well, we could yo-yo back and forth with that one for a little while, couldn't we?" Emmett replied. "I think you and I are going to get along, aren't we, Yo-Yo?"

"As long as you don't pull my string."

Emmett started to reply, but Gram was tired of all the foolishness.

"Emmett, just put the mail on the kitchen table," she interrupted.

The Strokowkis said good-bye and Kaden followed Gram into her cabin. Emmett had put the mail on top of the album cover and picked up a brochure sitting next to it. Kaden recognized the brochure. It had pictures of band instruments on the outside and inside was a rental form. Kaden had brought one home just like it but it had gone in the trash.

"It's getting pretty musical around here," Emmett said, putting the brochure in his shirt pocket. "Always good to have a little music in the house." He reached over and turned the record player back on.

"Playing a trumpet would be fun," Kaden said, "and educational, too." But from the look on Gram's face, Kaden knew it was pointless.

"Enough nonsense," Gram said. "Here's what I need from the Big Apple."

Kaden took the list and followed Emmett to his truck. As they drove away, he told Emmett all about the new kid.

When they reached town, instead of going to the Big Apple, Emmett turned onto the main highway.

"Where are you going?" Kaden asked. "I thought we were going grocery shopping."

"We'll do that later," Emmett said. "We need to take a little side trip to Chapston City first."

"What for?"

"I have to pick up some wood. The school sign was damaged this morning. They asked me if I would make another and we have some other errands to run there, too."

"What happened to the sign? Did Thredt kids vandalize it?"

"No, it wasn't Thredt this time but I'm not at liberty to say what happened. I'm sworn to secrecy."

"What else do you have to do in Chapston City?" Kaden asked.

"You'll see," Emmett said. An hour later, Kaden was walking out of the music store with a trumpet case in his hand.

"Don't tell Gram about it just yet," Emmett said. "I know I can talk her into it but it will take some time and you can't wait that long. Band will be starting and you need to start with them."

"How am I going to sneak a trumpet into my cabin?" Kaden asked. "And there's no way I can practice without her hearing me."

"I'll take it home with me," Emmett said. "You can pick it up when Doris stops for breakfast."

"What about in the afternoon?" Kaden asked. "And practicing?"

"I'll tell Gram I need you every day after school for a little while. Doris can let you off at my house. You know how it is.

Gram just needs a little sweet talk. I'm sure she'll sign you up for band in a few weeks. But until then it's just between us, okay?"

"Okay, thanks," Kaden said.

Sunday, September 4

CHAPTER TWELVE

ALLIES

Sunday morning broke bright and clear. With a cooler, some fishing rods, and a tackle box in the bed of the truck, Emmett and Kaden turned toward town.

"Where are you going?" Kaden asked. "The river's the other way."

"We're going to get Yo-Yo," Emmett said. "I called his mom and invited him to come along. I wanted to surprise you."

Kaden was excited his new friend would be with them but now his plans to talk with Emmett were thwarted. He was with Emmett yesterday afternoon but he never found a way to bring up Dad and the new backpack. When Emmett suggested going fishing, Kaden thought that would be the perfect time.

"That's okay, isn't it?" Emmett said when Kaden didn't immediately respond.

"It's a super surprise," Kaden said enthusiastically. "Thanks." And he really meant it. It would be fun to have Yo-Yo with them.

When Yo-Yo came bounding out of his house with a bright red duffel bag, Kaden learned there was a second part to Emmett's surprise. Yo-Yo would be spending the night at the cabins. Kaden scooted over, letting Yo-Yo in.

"This is so awesome. I've never been fishing before," Yo-Yo said as they drove out of town. Kaden smiled. He'd never had a kid spend the night.

One of the great things about fishing, Emmett always said, *is it gives you time to think*. And that's what Kaden did. As he cast his line and reeled it back in, he thought about how he and Emmett always got along. They went places and did things together and Emmett was an ally when trying to convince Gram of letting Kaden do things. It was Emmett who convinced Gram that Kaden could have a bike when he was five, could walk to the fire tower alone when he was eight, and could have a BB gun when he was nine. Kaden was sure Emmett had a hand in him getting to move to Cabin Two, and just yesterday Emmett set it up so he could be in band.

Kaden cast his line toward a deep pool formed by a fallen tree. The lure went a little too far and landed over a partially submerged tree trunk. He quickly popped it up and back before it could snag, reeled it in, and cast again, this time not quite as hard. The bright yellow rooster tail spinner plopped into the water just this side of the tree trunk. Right where Kaden wanted it. Almost instantly, a fish took the lure. Kaden set the hook and played the fish until he brought it in.

After he put the fish on the stringer, Kaden looked downstream. Emmett had watched him catch it and gave him a thumbs-up but Yo-Yo didn't seem to notice. He was standing near Emmett staring intently at a bobber floating out in front of him, as if he could will a fish to pull it under.

Kaden cast his line again and went back to his thoughts. There was an understanding between Emmett and Gram regarding his father. Kaden could talk to Emmett about anything on his mind. Anything except for the subject of Dad. Other than a few stories about when Dad was a kid, Emmett was silent on the subject. Even when letters came from the prison, Emmett only spoke to Gram about them. Deep down, Kaden knew even if Yo-Yo had not come along today, Emmett still wouldn't have said a word about his father.

Like always, he would have said, "If you want to know more about your dad, you'll have to ask your grandmother."

Suddenly Kaden heard Emmett yell, "Set the hook!" He looked downstream just in time to see Yo-Yo flip the fishing rod up so fast and hard, the bobber and hook flew out of the water, sailed backward over Yo-Yo's head, and got caught up in the bushes behind him. Kaden smiled, watching Yo-Yo and Emmett laugh as they untangled the hook from the bush. Kaden cast again, wondering if Yo-Yo would be someone he could talk to.

Would Yo-Yo really understand about my father? Kaden thought. *Yo-Yo has a whole family, with a mom and a dad, probably two sets of grandparents, and tons of aunts, uncles, and cousins. They live in a regular house. They own televisions, cell phones, and computers. The Strokowskis lead a normal life.*

Kaden heard Emmett and Yo-Yo splashing through the water, walking upstream to find another hole. *It was Yo-Yo who took the first step to be friends*, Kaden thought. *And he never made any mean comments like Luke. I was actually mean to Yo-Yo, but he wasn't mean back. In fact, he acted like the bus incident never even happened.* But Kaden wasn't sure he was ready to talk with Yo-Yo about his father.

Just before suppertime, they pulled into the circle drive. Gram was sitting on the porch shucking corn.

"What's he doing here?" Gram said when they all got out of the truck.

"You've met Yo-Yo. He's Kaden's friend and he's spending the night," Emmett stated.

"Says who?" Gram stood up and crossed her arms. Emmett took Gram by the elbow and guided her into the house. Kaden turned and rushed into Cabin Two, leaving Yo-Yo standing alone by the truck holding his duffel bag.

"Friends only get boys into trouble," Kaden heard Gram say over the intercom.

"Kaden's getting older. He needs to be around others his age," Emmett stated firmly. What Gram said next, Kaden didn't hear. The intercom had gone silent and the red light turned off.

Kaden went back out. Yo-Yo was still standing by the truck. Kaden grabbed the stringers of fish from the cooler.

"Come on," he said. "We're going in."

Together they stepped up onto the porch. As they reached Gram's door, Emmett stepped out and pulled the boys aside.

"Don't mess up," he warned quietly. "And do extra chores. Yo-Yo, you too."

The boys were on their best behavior all evening. They finished shucking the corn and set the table. As Gram fried the fish the two boys sat nervously on the couch, aware she was watching every move.

"Neither of you boys has done any reading today," Gram stated.

Yo-Yo was sitting next to the bookcase. He jumped up suddenly as if something had bitten him, grabbed the closest encyclopedia volume, and quickly opened it to a random page.

"Zoysia grass," he blurted out.

"What?" Gram said.

"Zoysia grass," Yo-Yo repeated, and read aloud as fast as he could. " 'A thick, tough kind of grass that's used to stop erosion and grows well in all sorts of conditions. It's used on many golf courses and parks because of its resistance to weeds.' " Yo-Yo looked up. "It tells all about it right here, in volume 18, W-X-Y-Z." Yo-Yo talked so quickly and nervously, even Gram had to smile. He sounded just like his mom when she tried to get Gram to sign Kaden up for band.

"Quick talkers," Gram said. "Must be a family trait."

Yo-Yo stopped talking but kept poring over page after

page of the encyclopedia with Kaden looking over his shoulder until dinner.

After dinner, the two boys worked together at Kaden's desk on the half-finished model airplane. Gram's voice came unexpectedly over the intercom. "Yo-Yo, you're welcome to come here anytime."

A few minutes later, the first notes of a song started playing through the intercom.

Kaden suspected putting on music was Gram's way of saying she wasn't listening in on them, and Kaden appreciated it. Three slow songs played. Then a lively song started up, first with a string of piano notes and soon joined by the strong beat of a guitar.

Kaden recognized it from the night before. Gram had played the rock-and-roll song over and over, saying it was one of her favorites. The music came through the intercom at full volume and Yo-Yo was dancing around the room, strumming an air guitar. Kaden pretended he was pounding on a keyboard but suddenly stopped. He knew what was coming next. Kaden put his hand up to tell Yo-Yo to stop, too. Yo-Yo looked questioningly at Kaden.

A male's voice joined the instruments, singing the first few lines of the song. Suddenly Gram's voice joined in, belting out lyrics, louder than the singer.

Yo-Yo was instantly rolling on the floor, laughing as Gram's gravelly voice continued to pour through the intercom. Kaden quickly grabbed his pillow, smothered the intercom, and, falling back onto the bed, laughed uncontrollably, too.

Late that night, Kaden lay in bed listening to the crickets and tree frogs through the window. Yo-Yo had quickly fallen asleep but Kaden couldn't. He lay there with his eyes shut, thinking. While fishing, he had made the decision to talk with Yo-Yo about his dad but there was one more thing worrying him. The fire tower. He hadn't told Yo-Yo about the tower and wasn't sure he wanted to. But he knew he couldn't talk to Yo-Yo in his room. Gram would hear through the intercom. The fire tower offered privacy but it was Kaden's special spot and no one but Gram and Emmett knew he went up there. Kaden's eyes suddenly popped open. *Except Dad,* he thought suddenly. *Dad knew! He left the backpack for me there.*

Kaden had not really thought about it before. *But Dad knew! Or did he?* In his mind, Kaden went over the day he first saw the white truck come up the fire tower road. He knew Dad hadn't seen him.

Then he thought about finding the backpack. *Maybe the backpack wasn't really for me. Maybe Dad threw it up there and was going to come back for it later.* Worry set in. *Maybe Luke was right. Maybe Dad was planning to hide stolen stuff in it in the woods.* Now Kaden was wide awake. He sat up in bed, looking out the window at the darkness. A crescent moon waxed in the sky. Just bright enough to make shadows. *No*, Kaden told himself. He was certain Dad wasn't like that anymore. He was positive Dad left the backpack for him. Kaden tried to convince himself but could not erase the conflicting thoughts from his mind. He looked over at Yo-Yo. Gram wouldn't talk with him about it and neither would Emmett but Kaden was glad to know he would soon have somebody to talk it over with.

Monday, September 5

CHAPTER THIRTEEN

CABIN FIVE

The next morning, Kaden, Yo-Yo, and Gram had just finished breakfast on the porch, when Emmett walked up from the road. It wasn't even seven o'clock.

"Everybody sleep well?" Emmett asked. Kaden got up and gave Emmett his seat. He knew Emmett was checking up on them to make sure everything had gone okay.

"I should think they got plenty of rest," Gram said. "I let them sleep in."

"All the way to six thirty," Yo-Yo complained.

"That late, huh?" Emmett grinned.

"I've got chores lined up for the boys to do after breakfast," Gram said. "No sense in wasting daylight."

"Now Greta," Emmett said. "It's Labor Day. A holiday. Give them a break. Let them just be boys for the day."

Kaden and Yo-Yo waited. Gram frowned at Emmett. Emmett smiled at Gram. "You're not going to turn into hoodlums in one day, are you, boys?" Emmett said.

"No, sir," Yo-Yo started. "Not us. Not hoodlums. We'll do a little reading and then . . ."

Kaden kicked Yo-Yo and gave his head an almost imperceptible shake. He didn't want Yo-Yo to list something they would do that Gram didn't believe in.

"Well, you can at least hang out the laundry. I already did a load this morning while you two were sleeping in," Gram stated.

"Come on," Kaden said. He and Yo-Yo walked toward Cabin Four.

"Did you ask him?" Kaden heard Emmett quietly say. "He never mentioned a word yesterday."

"No, there's nothing to ask," Gram answered. "You said the backpack didn't come from you, so there's only one person it could have come from. I don't know what Dennis is up to but I haven't seen him for over a week and I don't think Kaden has either."

"The boy's growing up, Greta," Emmett said. "You can't shelter him forever. You need to talk with him. Or let me."

"We've been over this before, Emmett."

Kaden wanted to hear the rest of the conversation, but Yo-Yo started talking. "Where are we going? I thought we had to do laundry."

"Cabin One is the junk cabin," Kaden started explaining. "It's like a basement, attic, and garage all rolled into one. Then there's my cabin and Gram's, and Cabin Four is the laundry room, or as Emmett likes to call it, the formal bath."

"What's in Cabin Five?" Yo-Yo asked.

They had reached the fourth cabin. Kaden ignored Yo-Yo's question, opened the door, and walked in. Yo-Yo followed him.

A washing machine stood in the back corner. A small table covered with a pink vinyl tablecloth sat beside it, holding two plastic laundry baskets. A bathtub and shower occupied the other back corner. A flowery pink shower curtain was pushed to one end and a fluffy pink throw rug was on the floor. A tall set of pink wicker shelves stood against the wall holding stacks of sheets, neatly folded pink towels, and a variety of knickknacks.

"Wow!" Yo-Yo said. "I wasn't expecting this. It's so . . . so girly."

"All the pink stuff is Emmett's doing," Kaden said, opening the washer, pulling out wet clothes, and putting them in one of the baskets. "Gram put in the bathtub and washer when we first moved here. From then on Emmett's added something for each birthday and Christmas. He says a woman needs at least one room that's womanly. Gram grouches about it but she hasn't thrown the stuff away. My guess is she likes it, even though she'd never admit it."

"I don't care for all the pink but I like the monkey," Yo-Yo said.

On the top shelf sat a ceramic monkey with its hands covering its mouth. Kaden knew it was Emmett's way of telling Gram he'd keep her secrets.

Kaden let the washing machine lid drop, picked up the loaded basket, and headed for the door. Yo-Yo followed but before Kaden pushed open the screen door, Kaden abruptly turned around. Yo-Yo walked right into the laundry basket.

Kaden asked, "Can you keep a secret?"

"Scout's honor."

"Good. When we finish with the laundry, I have something to show you."

After hanging the clothes up to dry, the two boys went to Kaden's cabin, grabbed his backpack, then rushed back to the kitchen.

"Fill the canteen with water and grab us each a couple juice boxes from the refrigerator," he told Yo-Yo as he made three peanut butter and jelly sandwiches. He stashed everything in his backpack and they stepped out onto the porch.

"You two are awfully quiet," Gram said. "What are you scheming?"

"Nothing," Kaden said. "We were just making some lunch to take to the tower. Is there anything we could have for dessert?"

"I don't think Emmett would mind if someone stole off with that bag of cookies out in his truck," Gram said, smiling.

"Cookies?" Emmett said innocently.

"Everyone knows you always keep a bag hidden behind the seat," Gram said.

Yo-Yo raced over to the truck, rummaged around, and came out with a half-full package of cookies. He crammed them into Kaden's backpack and then followed Kaden along the shortcut through the woods from the back of the junk cabin to the fire tower road.

"What were you talking about, going to a tower?" Yo-Yo asked.

"You'll see. It's a secret and you can't tell anyone about it," Kaden said.

They were quiet until they turned onto the tower road.

"You never told me what's in Cabin Five," Yo-Yo said.

Kaden had wondered how to start and was glad Yo-Yo

just stumbled into it.

"It's my dad's cabin," he said.

"But I thought . . . ," Yo-Yo started, then stopped.

"That's okay; it's no big secret my dad's been in prison," Kaden said. "Cabin Five was his cabin when he was a kid."

"Your dad lived here when he was a kid, too?" Yo-Yo asked.

"Just in the summer. My grandpa was the president of a big company in Chapston City but he loved to fish. So he always took the summer off and came up here to fish. At first Grandpa, Gram, and Dad all lived in the big cabin and rented the four little cabins to other fishermen. But when Dad turned ten, he got to move into Cabin Five by himself."

"I bet you miss your grandpa," Yo-Yo said.

"I never knew him. He died in a car wreck just before my dad started high school. After that Gram never came out here again, at least not until after I was born."

"So you've lived out here your entire life?" Yo-Yo asked.

"No, not until I was three. I lived with Gram in Chapston City. Dad was there at first but I vaguely remember him. Can't hardly picture what he looks like. He came and went, and then one day he never came back at all. I didn't know it then, but that's when he went to prison. After that Gram sold everything and we moved out here."

"What about your mom?" Yo-Yo said.

Kaden wasn't expecting this question. "She died when I was a baby and my dad just showed up at Gram's doorstep holding me. That's how I came to live with Gram. I've wondered about her but don't think my dad told Gram much about my mom. The only thing I've heard is her name was Katie. That's how I got my name. The first syllable is from her name, the second comes from Dennis, my dad's name."

"At least you don't have to explain your name every time you meet someone," Yo-Yo stated.

"Yeah, that must be a pain," Kaden agreed.

"You get used to it," Yo-Yo said.

They walked along for a little while longer.

"So, if your grandpa had a big company . . . ," Yo-Yo started, then hesitated. He kicked at a rock, but said nothing more.

"If he had a big company what?" Kaden said, not wanting Yo-Yo to stop with the questions. He was actually relieved to have a chance to talk about what was never discussed.

"If he had a big company, what happened to all his money? How come you can't afford a phone or TV?"

Kaden laughed. "Grandpa left Gram plenty of money. Everyone knows she could buy anything she wants. She just doesn't want to. She chooses to live like she does. And I guess

I'm stuck with living like she does, too."

"Wow. I don't think I could handle that."

"It's not so bad. I have just about everything I need."

"Except a phone and a TV," Yo-Yo said.

"And a bunch of other stuff," Kaden said, laughing. They walked on for a little while, laughing and listing all sorts of things that Kaden could need.

"So, is there any stuff in Cabin Five from when your dad was a kid?" Yo-Yo asked.

"I don't know. I've never been in there," Kaden said. "It's always locked. I've tried to look through the window but there's only a little crack between the curtains and I can't see much, just furniture."

"Wonder why your grandmother didn't let you move into Cabin Five instead of Cabin Two? You could have used all your dad's stuff. I've got a lot of my dad's stuff. His desk, his dresser, all his sports stuff, his bat and glove."

"I only have one thing that belonged to my dad. When I turned nine, Emmett went in Cabin Five and brought out a pair of binoculars. He said he gave them to Dad when Dad turned nine and thought I should have them."

"Didn't you go in with Emmett?" Yo-Yo asked.

"No, I wanted to but Gram made me wait on the porch. She said there was nothing in there but furniture. The conversation was over and the door was locked again."

"If there's nothing in there, I wonder why she won't let you go in," Yo-Yo pondered.

"Gram pretty much keeps me away from anything that has to do with my dad. Discussions, letters, even furniture. Maybe she's afraid I'll end up like him." Kaden kicked hard at a rock. It bounced up the road.

Yo-Yo reached the rock Kaden had kicked and nonchalantly took a turn kicking it. "Did the intercoms belong to your dad?" he asked.

"No. They're Gram's way of keeping her eye on me. Whenever I want to do something and Gram won't let me, her excuse is she didn't keep her eye on Dad enough. She doesn't say that to me, though. She says it to Emmett when she thinks I can't hear."

They walked on, taking turns at kicking the rock. When they reached the muddy patch, the stick was still standing upright where Kaden had left it.

"Look at this," Yo-Yo said. He started to pull the stick out of the mud.

"Leave it there. It lets me know if anyone has driven up the road," Kaden said as he inspected the patch. The leaves were uncrushed just as he had left them and no fresh tire tracks were in the mud. There were some raccoon tracks, though. Kaden pointed them out to Yo-Yo.

"How do you know they're raccoon prints?" Yo-Yo asked, leaning over to inspect them.

"They look like little hands," Kaden said. "And these are rabbit, with two longer marks in front and two shorter marks, one behind the other, in back."

"Ever seen any bear prints?" Yo-Yo asked.

"No, but Emmett has."

Yo-Yo looked all around. "I'd like to see one."

"Me too," Kaden said.

CHAPTER FOURTEEN

SECRETS

The boys reached the end of the road and stepped over the log barricade. As they walked up the short weedy path, Yo-Yo's eyes moved upward, following the steel beams of the fire tower until they reached the small room at the top. A crow jumped from a window. Flapping its wings, it zoomed like a torpedo, aiming straight toward them. The breeze from its wings ruffled Yo-Yo's hair as the glossy black bird sped just inches above his head. Yo-Yo jumped back so fast, he tripped and fell into a sticky briar patch with leafy vines weaving through the thorny branches.

"So, is that your secret?" he asked, pointing to the crow that landed on Kaden's head.

As Kaden leaned over to pull Yo-Yo out of the bushes, the bird jumped down onto his back, its feet grabbing hold of the crisscrossed cord on the backpack. When Kaden straightened back up, the bird hopped onto his shoulder, muttering in his ear.

"One of them," Kaden answered Yo-Yo. "Meet Kubla." Kaden swung the backpack around and pulled out the canteen.

"Is he your pet?" Yo-Yo asked.

"No, just a good friend. I rescued him when he was a baby. Now hold your hands out. I'll pour some water in them. I don't have any soap but water will be better than nothing."

"What for? There's only a couple of scratches and they're not really bleeding."

"What wasn't prickly was poison ivy," Kaden answered, nodding toward the vine-covered bushes. "If you wash it off real quick, you might not get any of it."

"Great," Yo-Yo said sarcastically. He grabbed the canteen and sloshed its entire contents over his arms and legs.

Kaden walked to the other side of the fire tower, disappeared into the dense foliage, and came out holding the coil of rope and rock.

"That's cool, a rock with a hole all the way through it," Yo-Yo said.

"It's a friendship rock. Emmett gave it to me."

"Where I used to live, friendship rocks had a different color line all the way around it, like a ribbon on a gift. What's the rope for?"

As if to answer his question, Kubla pushed off Kaden's shoulder and flew to the top of the tower, cawing the entire way. Yo-Yo looked at the tower and back to Kaden. "You don't mean . . ."

"Yep. That's another one of my secrets." Kubla cawed down to them. "He's telling me to hurry up."

"But how—" Yo-Yo started.

"It's easy. Watch."

Kaden launched the rock over the beam, climbed the rope to the landing, and yelled down, "Your turn."

Yo-Yo tried, but once he was a few feet off the ground, his efforts just made the rope swing. He dropped back down.

"I don't think I can!" he yelled up.

Kaden came back down the rope. "It took me a while to learn, too," he said. "Emmett had to hold the rope at first."

Kaden pulled the rope taut and stood on it. "Try again. It will be easier if it can't swing."

It took a while but Yo-Yo finally made it to the crossbeam. Kaden talked him through how to get on the landing and then climbed up again. He removed the rope from the crossbeam and coiled it over his shoulder.

"Why are you untying it? We're not going to jump down, are we?"

"No, but I don't want anyone to know we're up here."

"Who would come here?"

"Hikers," Kaden said, but as he started up the stairs he added under his breath, "and maybe my dad."

When they had climbed through the trapdoor, Yo-Yo went from one side to the next, looking out in all directions. "This is so awesome!" he said. "You can see forever up here."

Kaden thought about the first time he climbed up the tower. Emmett had brought a ladder and Kaden followed him, circling upward from landing to stairs, landing to stairs. When they reached the top, Kaden scrambled through the trapdoor and did exactly what Yo-Yo was doing.

As Yo-Yo peered out the windows, Kubla made soft chortling sounds, his black feet grasping one of the metal window frames. Kaden hung the rope on the peg and let the rock drop noisily to the floor. The bird half flew, half jumped to land on the rock. He stood there for a while, gurgling and muttering, then jumped to the floor. With both feet together, Kubla hopped halfway across the floor and picked up something with his beak. Then he strutted back, one foot in front of the other like a proud general. Opening his wings, he made a flying leap back to the window frame, where Kaden stood beside Yo-Yo. A matchstick was in the bird's beak.

"Watch this," Kaden said to Yo-Yo. He took the matchstick from Kubla and dropped it out the window. Kubla dove after it.

It was Kubla's favorite game, retrieving matchsticks. The bird's aviator stunts, barrel rolls, loops, and torpedolike plummets always fascinated Kaden. The bird tightly turned out of a dive and unbelievably came up with the matchstick grasped in his shiny black beak. Unless distracted, Kubla rarely missed his retrieve.

"That's so wicked!" Yo-Yo said. Kubla returned, landed on Kaden's head, and leaning over, held the matchstick in front of Kaden's eyes.

Kaden dropped the matchstick for Kubla again and sat down, leaning against the wall. He opened the backpack and took out two sandwiches and juice boxes. He handed a sandwich to Yo-Yo as Kubla flew back through the window. Kubla took one look at the open backpack, dropped the matchstick onto the floor, and hopped into the backpack. The backpack looked alive as the crow moved inside, and there was a muffled sound of the bird pecking at the cookie package.

It wasn't long before Kubla emerged from the backpack

with a cookie in his beak and darted quickly through the open window.

"He'll go over to the dead limb on that tree," Kaden said without standing up to look. But Yo-Yo watched attentively as the bird dove downward. Just as Kaden said, it landed on a large dead limb. The limb was near the top of the tallest tree but the tree reached only half the height of the tower.

"Crows can't hang on to things with their feet," Kaden explained. "He'll bite down and get a little bit but most of it will crumble and fall. Then he'll fly down to eat the pieces. When he's finished, he'll be back for another but I won't let him have any more."

Kaden wolfed down his sandwich and stood up. He went over to the metal chest, opened the lid, and dropped in the backpack. The lid slammed shut just as Kubla returned. Squawking, Kubla jumped up on the lid, then jumped to Kaden's shoulder and gave it a peck.

"Ouch! No!" Kaden exclaimed, pushing the bird off. "He's mad he doesn't get seconds," he told Yo-Yo.

Yo-Yo had been so engrossed watching Kubla, he'd only taken one bite of his sandwich. Before he knew what was happening, a flutter of wings came toward his hand. The bird grabbed at the sandwich and made his getaway, taking most of the sandwich with him.

Kaden laughed at Yo-Yo's startled expression. "Snooze, you lose," he said, "especially with peanut butter sandwiches. They're his favorite."

Yo-Yo looked toward the dead limb. Kubla stood with the bread hanging from his beak.

"That's why I made three," Kaden said. "I figured Kubla would get one somehow."

Kaden opened the chest again, pulled out the backpack, and tossed it to Yo-Yo. Yo-Yo reached into the backpack but quickly pulled his hand back out.

"Gross!" he exclaimed, holding up his hand. A thick gooey white glob covered his fingers. Kaden laughed.

"It's not funny," Yo-Yo said, but Kaden kept laughing.

"Give me your canteen."

"Won't do any good. You used up all the water washing off poison ivy but there's an old rag in there." Kaden pointed to the chest.

Yo-Yo opened the chest. "Wow, there's a bunch of stuff in here."

As Yo-Yo wiped off his hand Kaden carefully removed the extra sandwich and the bag of cookies from the backpack. He turned the backpack inside out and took the rag from Yo-Yo.

"It didn't get on the sandwich or the cookies," Kaden said as he wiped the bird's droppings from the backpack. With his index finger and thumb, Yo-Yo picked up a small corner of the sandwich's baggie and held it up for inspection. Satisfied, he ripped open the baggie and took a big bite.

Kubla flew back through a window. Yo-Yo turned his back on the bird but Kubla was undeterred. He reached over Yo-Yo's shoulder and tried to nab the sandwich. Kaden reached out and took hold of the bird. "You've had enough, you little pig. Let Yo-Yo eat."

Yo-Yo finished his sandwich and started rummaging through the chest. Pushing aside a book, a pad of paper, and a wadded-up T-shirt, he inspected an assortment of rocks and feathers. He picked up a turtle shell and then looked inside a small box, which held some dried butterflies and a cicada shell. On the bottom of the chest was a long, flat metal tool with a wooden handle. The metal was smooth on one side, but sharp pointy teeth completely covered the other side.

"What's this?" he said.

"It's a rasp. I'm making a walking stick for Gram." Kaden pointed to a long stick with a big knob of wood on one end leaning in the opposite corner of the tower. "I'll scrape it with the rasp until it's the right thickness for Gram's hand. Then I'll have to sand it smooth, and I'm going to carve a crow from that knob."

Yo-Yo put the rasp back, pulled out the binoculars, and

looked out the windows. Kaden sat back down on the floor, continuing to pet Kubla. Kubla made little gurgling noises of contentment, almost like a cat's purr.

"Emmett's pretty cool showing you how to get up here," Yo-Yo stated as he looked through the binoculars.

"Yeah, it was my tenth-birthday present from Emmett. Gram gave me Cabin Two with a set of intercoms, but Emmett gave me a secret hideout."

"So this," Yo-Yo said, waving his arm around the tower, "and that," he added, pointing to Kubla, "is your secret."

"Yeah," Kaden answered.

"How come you keep this a secret? If you told everybody, you'd be the kid with a tower, not the kid with the dad in prison."

"Can't. We're not really supposed to be up here. Emmett's a good friend of the sheriff's and he said it was okay if I didn't tell anyone. Besides, telling would only make things worse. Everyone knows the reason the stairs were removed."

Kaden said nothing more. He just continued petting Kubla, who had settled comfortably in his lap. Yo-Yo waited but when Kaden didn't explain, he finally said, "I don't."

Kaden poked the straw into his second juice box and slurped on it until the sides of the box collapsed inward. He tossed the empty box into a corner. The movement caught

Kubla's attention and he hopped over to inspect it.

"When they caught Dad stealing in Chapston City, they searched the cabins, too. They found stuff there but they also found a bunch of his stolen goods stashed up here. And that was the end of the bottom stairs."

"When they searched the cabins was it like on TV?" Yo-Yo asked excitedly. "Did they have those forensic guys and stuff?" He tossed his second empty juice box into a different corner. Kubla marched over to investigate it, too.

"I don't know. At the time, I didn't know about any of it, not about Dad stealing, getting caught, going to prison, none of that," Kaden said. "I was just three."

"So when did you find out?"

"In first grade. Luke told me. I used to play with him at school. Then he had this birthday party. That's when he told me."

"Figures it'd be Luke," Yo-Yo said, "but I can't believe he invited you to his party."

"He didn't. I found out about my dad when Luke told me I wasn't invited because his dad said my dad was a thief."

"So what did you do?"

"I didn't believe him. But I was upset I wasn't invited to the party and when I told Gram why, she was madder than a hornet. But she also told me it was true. She said my dad was in prison for stealing but it had nothing to do with me or anybody else. And that's about all she's ever said. All the rest I've picked up along the way. People talk a lot in Promise and they must think I'm deaf."

"What does Emmett say?"

"He's never told me much either. It's like this big secret."

"Well, I've noticed Luke isn't into secrets," Yo-Yo said.

"Yeah, he brings it up whenever he gets a chance. You want a cookie?" Kaden said, changing the subject.

Yo-Yo pointed to Kubla. "I don't think it's possible, not with that thief over there." The word "thief" had popped out without any thought and Yo-Yo instantly regretted it. But it didn't upset Kaden.

"He is a thief and a tricky one, too." Kaden laughed. "You just have to be trickier." Kaden pulled a straw from one of the empty juice boxes, waved it around to catch the bird's attention, and tossed it out the window. Kubla followed the straw and Kaden quickly opened the chest.

"And you gotta be quick," he said, cramming a whole cookie in his mouth.

Yo-Yo followed Kaden's example and while watching Kubla play fetch, the two boys finished off Emmett's cookies.

"Have you ever been in an airplane?" Kaden asked.

"Yeah. Why?"

"I guess it looks like this, doesn't it?"

"Only when you first take off. Soon the trees are just like a lumpy green blanket. Cars and trucks look like little toys and you can't see people at all. Not like this. From up here, people would look small but you could still see them pretty good, even without binoculars."

Kaden agreed. From here he was close enough to recognize someone walking up from the barricade. *Unless you're trying to recognize someone from a memory formed eight years ago when you were only three*, Kaden thought. He closed his eyes and tried to recall just a glimpse or a shadow from the past. But all he could picture was a stranger in jeans, work boots, a gray T-shirt, and a cowboy hat.

"There's one more secret," Kaden said hesitantly. "Something nobody in town knows yet. Just Gram, Emmett, and me." And he told Yo-Yo about the letter, the man with the white pickup truck, and his worries about the backpack.

Tuesday, September 6

CHAPTER FIFTEEN

TRUMPETS

As usual, Doris pulled into Emmett's drive in the morning. Unlike usual, Emmett was not in the kitchen. Instead, as Doris and Kaden stepped off the bus, he stuck his head out of the shop door at the end of the driveway.

"There are some blueberry muffins keeping warm in the oven," he called out. "And I already made coffee. Make yourselves at home."

Kaden told Doris about the fishing trip while they ate but Emmett never came in the house.

"I wonder what he's doing out there," Doris said. "I thought for sure he'd be coming in to join us." She looked at her watch. "We need to get going."

"I'll go see what he's up to. I have to get something anyway," Kaden said. "I'll meet you at the bus."

When Kaden rushed out to the shop he was surprised the shop door was locked. Emmett never locked his doors. Kaden could hear the table saw going and he pounded on the door until he heard the saw stop. Emmett stuck his head out an open window.

"I'm working on the school sign," he said. "You can't come in. Nobody gets to see it until it's up."

"I need my trumpet," Kaden said.

"Oh yeah. Wait right there." A few seconds later the door opened again, just wide enough for Emmett to hand Kaden the black case.

Kaden sat alone in the middle of Ms. Ales's classroom, his backpack on his desk, the black trumpet case beside his chair. It wasn't long before Yo-Yo came in.

"Sweet! You're going to get to be in band after all," Yo-Yo said, nodding at the black case.

"Yeah, I forgot to tell you. Emmett got it for me. Gram doesn't know anything about it, so don't say a word to her."

Yo-Yo just smiled and slapped his hand over his mouth.

First bell rang and students started entering the room. Elana noticed the trumpet case right away.

"How did you get that already?" she asked. "I didn't think anyone got their instruments until band today."

"I didn't order it through Mrs. Strokowski," Kaden told Elana. "I got it in Chapston City."

"He probably burglarized the music store," Luke sneered.

Elana ignored Luke's comment. "I'm going to play the clarinet. What are you playing, Yo-Yo?"

"Sax," Yo-Yo answered.

"How about you, Luke?" Elana asked.

"I didn't sign up for band. Only losers would wear one of those dumb band uniforms." As he said it, he gave the trumpet case a big kick. It skidded down the aisle just as Ms. Ales walked in.

"Whose is it?" she asked.

"Mine," Kaden answered.

"Rules are you're to take instruments to the music room when you arrive at school, not bring them into the classroom. You should have read that in the middle-school handbook. So go take it there now, please."

"Don't blame him, Ms. Ales. It's not his fault," Luke said. "Breaking the rules is a family trait, isn't it, Kaden? He's just following in his daddy's footsteps."

Ms. Ales ignored Luke, and Kaden said nothing. But as he walked to the music room he thought to himself, *I'm glad people in band are losers. Every Tuesday and Thursday there will be a whole hour I won't have to be around Luke.*

When Kaden got home from school, Gram was waiting on the front porch.

"What's this?" Gram said, holding up a piece of paper.

"It's my class schedule," Kaden said, puzzled by Gram's angry tone.

"I know that," Gram said. "What I want to know is what *this* is." Gram pointed to fifth period, the class right after lunch. Kaden thought she had figured out he had signed up for band against her wishes.

"Study hall," he answered.

"I can read," Gram said. "What I asked is what it *is*. What do you do in study hall?"

"Nothing really. It's in the cafeteria after lunch every day. You can get your homework done if you have any. Otherwise, you're supposed to read a book or something. But most of the kids just talk. It's kind of like recess in elementary; you just don't go outside. Middle school doesn't have recess. Study hall is our only break."

The minute he said "break," Kaden knew what would come next.

"What do you need another break for? You just had lunch. That's why they call it lunch break. And when did they forget homework means work at home? Has everyone totally forgotten the meaning of the English language?"

Kaden took a deep breath. When Gram got on a roll, there was no stopping her.

"I don't know, Gram. I don't make the rules. That's just the way it is."

"And you go to study hall every day?"

"You do if you're not in band. If you're in band, you only go to study hall on Mondays, Wednesdays, and Fridays. Band is after lunch on Tuesdays and Thursdays."

Gram stared at the schedule a while longer, then handed it to Kaden. All evening Gram sat muttering on the porch glider but said nothing more about it until Kaden was in his cabin for the night.

"Kaden," she said through the intercom, "sign up for band."

Wednesday, September 7

CHAPTER SIXTEEN

ALL RILED UP

When Kaden came in to eat breakfast, Gram was wearing her dress. It was her only dress and she hardly ever wore it.

"Why are you so dressed up? Did someone die?"

"No, I've got some business to do," was all Gram said, ignoring more questions from Kaden.

When Kaden got on the bus, Gram followed. Doris also asked Gram about the dress and got the same reply. So did Emmett. He served the ladies some apple turnovers, then made up some excuse about needing Kaden's help outside.

"What's up?" Emmett asked.

"I don't know. She was all riled up yesterday about study hall. But she solved the band problem."

"How's that?" Emmett asked.

"When she found out band meets the same time as study hall two days a week, she told me to sign up for band."

"Does she know you already have a trumpet?"

"No. I'll just give her the rental forms to sign tonight and she won't suspect a thing when I come home with a trumpet tomorrow."

When Kaden and Emmett went back inside, Gram was fidgety.

"When are you leaving?" she asked Doris.

"I've got another fifteen minutes," Doris said, pouring another cup of coffee. "If I left now, I'd be early and the kids wouldn't be outside yet. Everyone knows I get to each of my stops at the same time every day."

"What's the matter with parents these days? If you get there fifteen minutes early, it shouldn't matter. They should have their children ready and waiting."

"Then we'd be at the school early and the teachers wouldn't be there. They're always running late."

"Well, it's clear to me someone needs to get things straightened out at that school," Gram said. "I guess it has to be me. I'll be waiting in the bus."

"The bus?" Doris, Emmett, and Kaden all asked at the same time.

"Of course," Gram answered. "I'm going to the school. How else would I get there?"

"The school?" they all three said in unison again.

"Isn't anyone listening this morning? I have business to do at that school and I'm taking the bus."

"You can't, Gram. Doris brings you to Emmett's but you can't go to school on it." Kaden shot Emmett a look of panic. Not only was he horrified about what kids would say if Gram was on the bus, but he was also worried about whatever business she had in mind.

"He's right," Emmett agreed. "I'll drive you and we can talk about whatever's upsetting you."

But Gram was not to be swayed. "Emmett, there's no need to waste your gas when my tax dollars fill that bus tank." Having stated her opinion, Gram walked out the door and onto the bus.

Doris drove down to town without saying a word. Gram was also silent and Kaden knew better than to say anything. As students piled into the bus, they took one look at Gram sitting in the first seat and they became silent, too. The only one who spoke was Luke and he only whispered.

"What's your old woman on here for?" Luke said, leaning over the seat from behind Kaden. "Afraid to ride the bus by yourself?"

Kaden looked at Gram to see if she heard. She didn't appear to but that usually didn't mean anything. He also realized Yo-Yo had been right. With Luke sitting behind him, Luke could quietly lean forward and whisper in his ear and nobody would hear a word. *I think another move is needed*, Kaden thought.

When they got to school, Gram told Doris to pull into the cars-only drive so she could go in through the front doors like a civilized person. Watching from his seat, Kaden saw Gram hurrying into the school, intent upon her mission.

Kaden could hardly concentrate on history, knowing Gram was somewhere in the building. Just before the bell rang ending first period, the door opened. There stood Mr. Price. Gram stood erect slightly behind the principal. Mr. Price informed Ms. Ales there would be a school-wide faculty meeting after lunch, during study hall. Kaden looked at Gram. Her mouth tightened at the words "study hall," but otherwise he could not read her face.

After lunch, the cooks wiped the tables as all fifty-seven sixth, seventh, and eighth graders reported to study hall. Teachers usually took turns being on duty for study hall but today no teachers were around. Instead, the secretary, the janitor, and the school nurse stood clustered by the door.

Under the unusual circumstances, the students were quiet at first, but gradually the cafeteria filled with the usual din of voices that grew increasingly louder. Kaden looked around. There were only three students who actually had books open. Worrying Gram might show up at any minute, Kaden quickly opened a book and advised Yo-Yo he should as well. But Gram never appeared. The bell rang and the sixth graders went to Mr. Clary's class. Mr. Clary said nothing about the meeting. Nor did any other teacher the rest of the day.

Gram was not on the bus when Kaden got on that afternoon.

"Do you want me to go find Gram?" Kaden asked Doris. "Or are you picking her up at the front doors?"

"I already took her home," Doris answered. "About two o'clock, I'd guess. Isn't that when the mail comes?"

"The mail?" Kaden asked.

"Yeah, I saw Mr. Schmerz leave your driveway just as I came around the bend," Doris said.

"Our driveway?"

"Yeah, I thought it was kind of odd but kept my mouth

shut. Didn't figure it was a good time to say anything, the way your grandmother was today."

"You sure it was Mr. Schmerz?"

"Who else has a white pickup?" Doris said. "I was just glad it turned the other way so your grandmother didn't see him. She's on enough of a warpath already."

Before Kaden could say more, the bus was swarmed with students. Kaden rushed to a seat, this time in the very back of the bus so he could keep an eye on Luke.

All afternoon, the students speculated about what had occurred between Mr. Price, the teachers, and Kaden's grandmother. Kaden was continually asked what it was about, and although he knew no more than the rest of them, rumors had been building. Now Luke added to them by loudly reporting he saw the sheriff's car in the parking lot and Sheriff O'Connor was looking closely at the broken sign.

"It's obvious Kaden had something to do with the vandalism," Luke said above the din. "So they called in his grandma and the sheriff. Wonder if they'll send you to juvie? Or maybe they'll let you share a prison cell with your father."

Although the back of the bus grew even louder with more speculation, Doris said nothing until Kaden was stepping off the bus.

"Don't worry about them. Everyone knows you had

nothing to do with the sign. Luke's just up to his usual troublemaking."

Between Gram's visit to the school and now Luke's accusation, Kaden was about to explode. He charged into his room ready to slam his backpack on his bed but stopped cold. Lying on his bed was a new baseball and glove.

Kaden stared at them. He knew Doris hadn't seen Mr. Schmerz's truck. Doris had seen Dad's. There was no doubt the ball and glove were for Kaden, and their presence put to rest the nagging thought that had been pestering him. The backpack had definitely been left for him, too.

Thursday, September 8

CHAPTER SEVENTEEN

HOME ALONE

Gram didn't say a word to Kaden about her visit to the school but went around all evening with a satisfied look on her face. The next morning as Kaden ate his breakfast, she signed the trumpet rental forms. Everything seemed back to normal until after school when Doris dropped Kaden off at the cabins. Gram was waiting on the porch. She was wearing her dress again.

"Could you drop me off at Emmett's on your way back to town?" Gram asked.

"Sure," Doris said. "What's up?"

"Emmett has to get the new sign set up and I'm going with him. The school board is meeting tonight and I need to be there," Gram said. "Kaden, no going to the tower while I'm gone. I'll be home late, so make yourself dinner."

After Gram left, Kaden took out his trumpet. In band that day, Mrs. Strokowski showed him how to hold the instrument.

"Now, keep the corners of your lips tight, the front of your mouth flat, and don't puff out your cheeks," she said.

Kaden put the horn to his lips and blew. It sounded like an elephant blast but Mrs. Strokowski seemed pleased.

"I want you to aim for consistency. Do you play baseball?"

Kaden nodded, wondering what that had to do with the trumpet.

"Well, practicing for a pure tone is like trying to pitch consistently over home plate. You have to practice the same throw over and over to get it there every time."

Now sitting on the porch, Kaden put the trumpet to his lips. Blast. Blast. Blast. He put the trumpet down and rubbed his mouth. Then he tried again. Practicing until his mouth grew tired, he went inside, made a sandwich, and headed for his cabin.

Kaden picked up his new ball and glove and went out behind his cabin. Several summers ago, Emmett had stretched a net between two trees at the edge of the woods. He'd painted a red square in the middle of it. Forty-six feet from the net, the exact distance on a Little League field, he'd made a pitcher's mound.

Kaden stood on the mound and pitched the ball toward the square. It hit dead center and bounced back at him, landing in the new glove. He pitched again and again, sometimes aiming at the center, sometimes at a specific corner.

It was almost dark when Kaden heard a vehicle pull in the circle drive and stop. The motor turned off and a door slammed. Pitching another ball, Kaden realized something wasn't right. If Emmett turned off the motor, he should have heard two doors shut. Gram's and Emmett's. If Emmett were just dropping Gram off, only one door would shut, but Emmett wouldn't have turned off the motor.

Kaden turned to look at the back of Gram's cabin. No lights lit up the curtains hanging in her bedroom window. He stood silently and listened. He heard no voices. Putting the ball in the glove, Kaden crept quietly between his cabin and the junk cabin and peeked around the corner. In the driveway was his father's white pickup truck.

Kaden instinctively pulled his head back out of sight and leaned against the side of his cabin, his heart beating wildly. He listened for footsteps in the gravel but all he heard were crickets. Cautiously, he peeked around the corner again and saw something quite clearly. His cabin was dark. Gram's cabin was dark. Cabin Four was dark. But light poured out the open door of Cabin Five.

Kaden pulled his head back again. The sun had still been out when he fixed a sandwich in Gram's cabin, so he hadn't turned on any lights. He hadn't turned on the light in his cabin either. *Dad doesn't think anyone is home*, Kaden realized. Kaden looked down at the ball and glove. They had been left on his bed when Gram had gone to the school and no one was home. And the backpack had been left at the tower before Kaden got home from school. Another thing was beginning to be quite clear. Dad was keeping watch on the place. He knew when they were there and when they weren't. *Except this time, Dad was wrong.*

Gathering up his courage, Kaden ran down the side and across the back of his cabin, across the back of Gram's cabin, past the back of Cabin Four, and then across the last gap to the back of Cabin Five. He listened but couldn't hear anything except his own breathing. Slowly, quietly, Kaden inched his way along the side of Cabin Five until he reached the front corner.

There, he stopped and listened again. He heard a drawer open and someone rummaging through its contents. Holding his breath, Kaden tiptoed around the corner and peeked into the crack between the curtains. A man was going through the desk drawer, his back to the window. The man shoved the desk drawer closed and turned toward the door. Kaden quickly ducked, getting only a glimpse of the man's face before he bolted around the corner and back behind Cabin Five.

"Is somebody out there?" Kaden heard the man call out. He heard footsteps crunching in the gravel of the circle drive. They went about ten steps, just about halfway between Cabin Five and Cabin Four, then stopped.

Kaden froze, saying nothing. The man stood still and said nothing. It was only for a few seconds but it seemed like forever. Finally Kaden heard the man say to himself, "Must have been a deer." Then the man walked back into the cabin.

Kaden didn't dare go look through the curtains again. He leaned back against the cabin wall, shut his eyes, and let out his breath. His hands were shaking with the realization that he had seen his father's face for the first time in years. Kaden thought his face looked familiar in a vague sort of way. *Probably because of the photos on Emmett's wall*, Kaden thought. *Dad would look older now, but he was still the same person, he would still look kind of the same, kind of familiar.*

Kaden wondered what his father was doing inside and why he was sneaking around, waiting for no one to be home. He was lost in his thoughts when he heard the door to Cabin Five close. He laid flat on his stomach and peeked around the corner. It was too dark to see much, just the silhouette of his father in the moonlight walking down the driveway. Soon he walked out of sight. Kaden got up and quietly scooted across the gap between the cabins. He looked around the far corner of Cabin Four and watched his father again, until he walked out of sight in front of Gram's cabin.

Kaden waited. He didn't hear anything. His father's truck was in front of Gram's cabin but he didn't hear the motor start.

Maybe he's sitting on the porch, Kaden thought. He listened intently but didn't hear the glider creak. He waited a little longer, wondering if he should sneak up to see what was happening, wondering if he wasn't just being a coward for not letting his father know he was there all along. He had almost talked himself into confronting his father when he heard the truck door close and the motor start. Headlights flooded the circle drive and Kaden watched the truck drive past the gap between Cabin Four and Gram's cabin. Then he ran to the front corner of Cabin Four just in time to see the truck turn left and head toward town.

Kaden walked down the drive to Cabin Five. The cabin was dark now and Kaden couldn't see anything through the crack in the curtains. He turned the knob on the door. It was locked. With a sigh, he went back up the drive to Gram's cabin. As he opened her door, something dawned on him.

Dad had a key to Cabin Five, he thought. Kaden turned on the light and sat down, wondering how his dad got a key. *Gram must have given him one the day Emmett took me to Pillie's. The day he wasn't ready to meet me.*

Normally, being alone at the cabins didn't bother him. But now, knowing Dad had been there, the silence made him nervous. Kaden got up, turned on all the lights, and randomly pulled out an album from under the kitchen sink. The album cover had a photo of a guy sitting at a table, playing a guitar.

Kaden put the record on. The first song on the album didn't do much for him but the next song was about a friend that sticks with you even when things are going bad. The guy called them rainy-day friends. The song made him stop thinking about his father and start thinking about Yo-Yo. He didn't know him very well but Yo-Yo seemed like the type of guy who would be both a rainy-day and sunny-day friend.

As the album played, Kaden searched through the cupboards for anything at all that could be considered dessert. He pulled out a box of raisins and the peanut butter. He scooped a big glob of peanut butter into a bowl and put a handful of raisins on top.

Kaden hadn't been paying attention to the lyrics of the third song but suddenly a line registered in his head. Leaving the bowl on the counter, he went back over to the record player, carefully picked up the arm, and gently set the needle in the wider groove just before the third song.

Kaden played the song over and over. It talked about needing time and about trust and faith. About being confused and trying to figure things out. The song hit home. Kaden felt confused and was trying to figure it all out. He needed time, and trust, and faith. *Maybe Dad is just like me. Maybe Dad needs those things, too.* Kaden decided he'd give Dad time. He'd wait until Dad was ready.

Kaden started the song over one last time and sat down with his peanut butter and raisins. He had taken only a bite when he heard a vehicle pull in and drive up to Gram's cabin. His heart started racing but he decided if it was Dad again, this time he wasn't going to hide. Kaden took a deep breath and went to the door. A blue truck sat idling in front of the cabin. Emmett's blue truck. Kaden stood at the door while Gram got out, said good night, and came inside.

"It took a while, but I got that school all straightened out," she stated matter-of-factly, smiling at Kaden. Gram seemed to be in a good mood and Kaden didn't want to say anything to rile her up again. He decided he wouldn't tell Gram that his father had been there that night.

Kaden said good night and went to his cabin. The music was coming through the intercom. Without turning on the light, Kaden walked across the room in the dark, turned on the bathroom light, and brushed his teeth. Then turning off the bathroom light, he crossed the room to his bed. When he pulled back the quilt, he heard something drop onto the floor. He walked back to his desk and turned on the light. On the floor was a small photo album. On the cover it said, "Photos for Father."

Kaden opened the album and looked at the first picture. He had seen it before. Emmett had a copy of that photo on the wall. A baby picture of him in a crib. He turned the page. The next picture he had seen before, too. He was sitting in a high chair, a cake with one candle in front of him. Opposite that picture was one of him astride a plastic horse on wheels. That baby toy was now in a back corner of the junk cabin.

Kaden flipped the page. There was only one more picture and it instantly made him catch his breath. He was about two years old and he was sitting on a man's lap. His dad's lap. Kaden was laughing in the photo.

Kaden sank down to the floor. A song played softly through the intercom as tears rolled down his cheeks. In the photo, his father was looking at him with the proud and loving look Kaden had longed to see from his dad for as long as he could remember.

Friday, September 9

CHAPTER EIGHTEEN

THE SIGN

Kaden didn't know how long he stared at that photo, but the next thing he knew, birds were chirping and sunlight was streaming in through the curtains. He opened his eyes. He was lying on the floor, the desk lamp still on and the photo album opened to the fourth picture. Kaden took one more look at the photo, closed the album, and raising up his mattress a little, slid it under.

When he went into Gram's for breakfast, Gram was in her dress again. But it didn't surprise Kaden this time. The dress had nothing to do with study hall. It was because of the sign.

Gram got on the bus with Kaden.

"I wouldn't normally be going," Gram told Doris. "I'm

sure I'd see that sign sooner or later but Mr. Price personally asked me to join him this morning at the unveiling."

Red flags went up in Kaden's mind. He suspected Mr. Price's invitation had nothing to do with the sign and everything to do with Gram's recent uncharacteristic visits to the school.

When they got to Emmett's, he was waiting by his truck.

"Sorry, folks," Emmett said as Doris opened the bus door, "but Greta and I have to get going. We need to be at the school before everyone else. It's a beautiful morning, so I left muffins, coffee, and juice for you two on the picnic table out back." Kaden was relieved Gram wasn't insisting on riding the bus to school again.

At school, instead of pulling around to the back, Doris pulled into the cars-only drive. All the students, middle school and elementary, piled off the bus and crossed to the grass strip. The teachers and a good many townsfolk had gathered there, too.

The new sign stood covered with a large tarp where the old sign had been. Beside the covered sign stood Emmett. He was grinning. Beside Emmett was Mr. Price. He was smiling. And next to the principal was Gram. Gram's lips were perfectly straight.

Kaden searched the crowd and found Yo-Yo. He was dressed in an old faded band uniform, holding a bugle.

"What's with the band uniform?" Kaden asked.

"Part of the program. Did Gram tell you anything about what's going on?"

"No, how 'bout your mom? Did she say anything?"

"No, but I got inside information."

"Really? How?" Kaden asked.

"I had to go with Mom to the school board meeting last night to model new band uniform possibilities."

"You're kidding," Kaden said.

"No. It was so embarrassing. I don't mind wearing a band uniform when you're playing in a band, but modeling? Give me a break."

"So, what's the inside scoop?"

But before Yo-Yo had a chance to say anything, the earsplitting squeal of a microphone got everyone's attention. All talking stopped.

"Students, will you please stand for the raising of the flag," Mr. Price's voice came over the loud speakers.

"That's my cue," Yo-Yo said. "Gotta run." Yo-Yo hurried to stand beside the flagpole.

As the flag was raised, Yo-Yo put the bugle to his mouth and started playing reveille. Kaden was impressed. A few notes were slightly off-key but nothing like the elephant blasts he made on his trumpet. Then Mr. Price invited Gram to lead the audience in the Pledge of Allegiance. Gram stood straight and solemn as she spoke through the microphone. When finished, the elementary teachers got the younger students seated in the grass as Mr. Price started speaking again.

"Good morning, students and teachers," he said, "and a big Promise Elementary and Middle School welcome to all the townsfolk. It's great to see you are interested in the education of our youngest citizens. I hope you will remain so when we ask to pass a bond next election."

"Enough with the campaigning!" someone yelled. "We're just here to see the sign." The crowd chuckled.

Mr. Price was not rattled. "We'll get to that, Clarence, just be patient. First, I have an announcement. Mrs. McCrory has brought it to our attention we could make better use of the students' time here at Promise Middle School. She has graciously helped us design a new program and will be funding it, too. The faculty and I met this week to work out the details and the board approved it last night. We've named the program C.A.R.E., which stands for *Citizenship and Responsibility for Everyone.*"

"Some of us didn't *care* for it," Luke's father called out from the crowd.

Mr. Price ignored Mr. Woodhead and continued. "As Mrs. McCrory pointed out, students should have responsibilities as citizens of our school community. C.A.R.E. will be on Mondays, Wednesdays, and Fridays after lunch instead of study hall. So, students, homework assigned on those days will be done at home. Band will continue as it is, after lunch on Tuesdays and Thursdays. Those not in band will go to study hall those two days as usual. Those students in band will no longer have study hall at all."

Audible complaints rose from the students. Kaden glanced at Gram, worried she might grab the microphone and ask them what part of the word "homework" they didn't understand. Much to Kaden's relief, Gram stayed put but the straight line of her lips turned down as she glared at the noisy students.

"Quiet down, students," Mr. Price instructed sternly. "During C.A.R.E., each middle-school grade level will be assigned one of three duties for the week. The duties will rotate each week to a different grade. One duty will be the School Beautification Duty. After lunch, students will stay in the cafeteria to empty trash, sweep the floor, and help wipe and fold the tables. Then they will go outside to pick up trash, rake leaves, and, especially, work on the beautification of the inner courtyard."

"What if it's raining?" Luke called out.

"If the weather is bad, you can help with inside chores," Mr. Price answered without hesitation. "Another duty will be Elementary Duty. Students will be assigned to each of the elementary classrooms to help that teacher in any way she sees fit. The third duty will be Library Duty. Students will help Ms. Ales check in and shelve books. The school board, as well as the faculty and I, wish to thank Mrs. McCrory for her insight and financial support in helping our students be a more responsible group of young citizens."

The audience politely applauded. The corners of Gram's mouth raised a little so it returned to a straight line, and she gave one nod.

When the applause ended, Clarence yelled out again, "What about the sign?"

"Okay, Clarence," Mr. Price said. "As most of you know, our school sign was accidentally destroyed."

"How?" Clarence interrupted.

Mr. Price chuckled and glanced at Doris. "You want to tell them?"

Doris turned beet red. "Everyone's going to know sooner or later," she said. "I hit the sign practicing for the State School

Bus Safety Days Competition."

The crowd roared.

"Okay, folks, quiet down," Mr. Price said. "Accidents happen, but you all know our children are in the safest of hands when they step onto a Promise school bus."

"Let's see the new sign!" Clarence interrupted again.

"All right, Clarence. You ready, Emmett?" Mr. Price asked.

Emmett nodded and picked up one corner of the tarp. Mr. Price picked up the other, and together, they lifted the tarp up and over the sign. The crowd loved it. Even Gram smiled as Mr. Price read the sign aloud.

"Promise Elementary and Middle School, where a Promise is stronger than a Thredt."

When the ceremony was over, Kaden and Yo-Yo joined the flow of students streaming through the front doors.

"There's something I need to tell you about but I don't want to here," Kaden said. "Do you think you can come to the cabins tomorrow? We'll go to the tower."

"Probably. I'll go ask Mom."

Yo-Yo turned right to head toward the music room. Kaden turned left. He was almost at Ms. Ales's room when

Luke and Elana came up behind him.

"Since when did your grandma know what's best for everybody?" Luke said over Kaden's shoulder. Kaden ignored him and kept on walking but Luke darted around in front of him and blocked his way.

"Are you going to answer my question or just sneak away like a thief?" Luke said, giving Kaden a hard shove. Kaden stumbled backward, knocking into Elana. Elana's books flew out of her hands and skidded in all directions.

"You need to watch where you're going," Luke sneered, but then turned to Elana and in a sweet, overly concerned voice asked, "Are you okay?"

Kaden started to pick up one of Elana's books but Luke kicked his hand away and put his foot down on top of the book.

"Did Elana ask for your help?" Luke said.

Kaden stood back up, leaving the book on the floor under Luke's foot. Mumbling "sorry" to Elana, Kaden tried to dart around Luke but Luke was faster. He slammed Kaden into the lockers and pinned him there.

"I'm not lifting a finger for your grandma's C.A.R.E. program. And you and your little punk friend better not rat me out or you'll regret it," Luke snarled into Kaden's face. "That's a promise."

Yo-Yo had come up and now stood behind Luke but out of his reach. "Sounds like a threat to me," he said. Luke let go of Kaden and turned toward Yo-Yo.

"What happened to your cute little band uniform?" Luke taunted.

"Come on, Luke," Elana interjected. "Let's just go eat breakfast."

But Luke didn't let up. "He looked just like a little munchkin, didn't he, Elana?"

"Actually, I thought so, too," Yo-Yo spoke up as if he didn't realize it wasn't a big joke. "Those uniforms are probably older than *The Wizard of Oz*. But that's the last anyone will see of them. The band's getting new ones." Yo-Yo nonchalantly leaned over and picked up one of Elana's books and handed it to her.

"Really?" Elana said, taking the book. "What do they look like?"

"Who cares," Luke stated. "Come on, Elana." Luke walked down the hall toward the cafeteria. Elana continued talking with Yo-Yo while Kaden picked up the rest of her books. But when Luke got to the back hallway, he called out, "I told you to come on, Elana."

Elana hesitated, then turned to Yo-Yo. "I'd better go or he'll get even madder."

CHAPTER NINETEEN

fRIENDSHIP ROCK

C.A.R.E. started that afternoon, and after lunch all the sixth graders gathered around the library checkout counter.

"There's not much to do, just those books to stack," Ms. Ales stated, pointing toward a half-empty book cart behind the counter. "So if a couple of you volunteer to put them away, I guess the rest of you can spend your time quietly talking, reading, or looking for a book to check out."

A couple of girls raised their hands to volunteer. Kaden did, too.

Luke made a point to push up next to Kaden.

"Only girls volunteer," Luke said, "and cowards. You're afraid of your own grandma, aren't you?" Luke gave Kaden a sharp jab in the ribs with his elbow, then headed toward the back of the room.

Not afraid, Kaden thought, rubbing his ribs. *Just smart.* He knew Gram would ask what they did in C.A.R.E. She wouldn't be too pleased if he said they just talked. He wouldn't be lying if he said *he* stacked books. He would just fail to mention only two other kids stacked them, too. As Kaden headed toward the book cart, Ms. Ales spoke up again.

"On second thought," she said, "I think everyone should participate in C.A.R.E. So, each of you take two or three books and put them in the proper places. Remember fiction is in alphabetical order by last name and nonfiction is filed by the Dewey decimal system. Then you can do as you please."

Everyone but Luke took some books. As they were placing the books on the shelves, Coach Dosser and the seventh graders came in carrying rakes and black plastic trash bags. They walked through the library and exited into the courtyard for School Beautification Duty.

"I wonder what will be left for us to do out there next week," Kaden said to Yo-Yo as he put his last book on the shelf. "The courtyard isn't that big."

"I don't know," Yo-Yo said, "but come on. I've been waiting for a chance to give you this all day." Yo-Yo headed toward a table. He pulled a plastic bag out of his backpack and dumped out the contents.

"What's all this stuff for?" Kaden asked, sitting down beside Yo-Yo and picking up a rock with a line all the way around it. There was an old portable CD player with a set of earbuds plugged into it, a dozen or so CDs in their plastic cases, a package of AAA batteries, a thin board about twelve inches long and three inches wide, a throwaway camera, a cell phone, a ziplock bag filled with sunflower seeds, a tiny blue LED flashlight, and a round plastic container of baby wipes.

"That's a friendship rock and the rest is a survival kit," Yo-Yo said. Then he whispered, "For the tower."

"Baby wipes?"

"They're antibacterial in case of random crow poop. Or," Yo-Yo said, raising his T-shirt to show a rash across his stomach caked with dried-up pink lotion, "to fend off attacks of poison ivy."

Kaden grinned. "What about all the other stuff?"

"First," Yo-Yo said, "the tower needs a name." He picked up the thin board and turned it over. Dark black letters spelling UDANAX were burned into the other side. Before Yo-Yo could explain, Luke sauntered up with Elana tagging close beside. Kaden heard Elana whisper, "Come on, Luke, just leave them alone," but Luke ignored her. Standing behind them, Luke reached between Kaden and Yo-Yo and picked up the CD player.

"Rob an antique store lately?" Luke laughed, letting the earbuds dangle from their cords in front of Kaden's face.

Kaden slumped in his seat, staring down at the table, his fist tightening onto the rock in his hand. His face turned beet red but he was silent. Still holding the CD player, Luke grabbed the small flashlight.

"Looks like part of a burglar's equipment to me," he said. "Is this so you can see what you're stealing?" Luke turned the light on and leaned over to shine it in Kaden's face. Again Kaden said nothing. He just turned his head away so the light wasn't in his eyes.

Luke pocketed the flashlight and reached for the baby wipes. But before he could say another word, Yo-Yo forcefully pushed his chair backward, hitting Luke hard in the shin.

"Hey, watch what you're doing, punk," Luke said, but Yo-Yo was quick. As Luke leaned forward to rub his shin, Yo-Yo jumped up and grabbed the CD player from him.

"That happens to be my mom's," he told Luke. "And before you call someone a thief, there's something in your pocket that doesn't belong to you. I'd like it back." Yo-Yo stepped right up to Luke, his hands on his hips. He was as face-to-face with Luke as he could get, considering Luke was a whole head taller.

"What are you going to do, teacher's brat? Go crying to your mommy?" Luke said, also putting his hands on his hips. "Besides, who's to say it isn't mine?"

"Elana is," Yo-Yo said. Luke looked at Elana.

"I gave it to Yo-Yo yesterday," she said quietly. "His mom brought him in after school for a Jumbo Lightning Moo-Cream."

"That's right," Yo-Yo said. "Prepayment for trying on band uniforms for the school board."

"Big deal. I have one of those flashlights, too," Luke said. "In fact, just about every kid in town does. You should know that, Elana. No way to tell this one isn't mine."

"All the other flashlights are purple," Elana said. "That was the only blue one."

"It's unique, like me," Yo-Yo said, grinning.

Elana giggled. Luke ignored Yo-Yo and glared at Elana. "Why'd you give him a special flashlight?"

"It wasn't anything special. I just pulled a flashlight out of the box, and it was blue," Elana said. "Must have gotten in there by mistake at the factory."

"Well, your mistake is you gave it to that little punk," Luke said, then turned to Yo-Yo. "And your mistake was ever coming to this school. If I see you in Pillie's again, it will be an even bigger mistake."

"From what I hear, you're banned. You'll only see me from the outside looking in," Yo-Yo said. He put his hand out. "Now, my flashlight, please."

"You still can't prove it's not mine," Luke said.

"Oh, stop it, Luke. Just give it back to him," Elana said.

"So, you want to be friends with these babies?" Luke said. "Look, they even bring their baby wipes to school." Luke gave the container a shove. It turned over and rolled off the table.

"All I said was give it back to him," Elana said. Yo-Yo still had his hand out.

Luke glared at Elana a while longer, then pulled the flashlight out of his pocket. He slapped it down in Yo-Yo's outstretched hand and stomped off. Irritated at Luke, Elana huffed off in the opposite direction.

"I tell you, she's not too bad if you can get her away from Luke," Yo-Yo said, watching her leave. "We're getting her turned around, just have to be patient."

Kaden said nothing but continued staring straight down at the table, head still bowed. Every muscle in his face was tense and taut. Yo-Yo stopped talking and began stuffing everything back into the plastic bag.

"Hey, snap out of it. You just have to learn to stick up

for yourself," Yo-Yo finally said to Kaden. "Luke is mostly all bark and he barks the most in front of Elana. You saw what he does. If you stand up to him, he puts his tail between his legs and runs. Just like a dog. That's what you have to think, he's just like a dog."

Yo-Yo started barking, then howling and acting like he was chasing his tail. Kaden finally had to grin.

"A big, mean dog," Kaden said as he picked up the baby wipes and handed them to Yo-Yo.

"No, a tall, skinny, mean dog," Yo-Yo said, grinning back.

The bell rang, ending C.A.R.E. for the day. Yo-Yo handed the plastic bag to Kaden.

"Thanks," Kaden said.

"No big deal. I'll tell you what the rest of the stuff is for tomorrow."

Kaden rolled the friendship rock around in his hand. "I wasn't saying thanks for the stuff," he said. "I was saying it for, well, you know, for sticking up for me."

"I'm not afraid of dogs," Yo-Yo said. "You just have to act bigger, look meaner, and bark louder."

Saturday, September 10

CHAPTER TWENTY

UNEXPECTED VISIT

It was hot for the second weekend of September. Not a breath of air, even above all the trees. Kaden and Yo-Yo dumped the stuff from the survival kit on the tower floor in front of them. Kaden hadn't brought up what he wanted to talk about and Yo-Yo hadn't pried.

"The sign," Yo-Yo said, picking up the thin board that said UDANAX. "Every hideout needs a name. Have you figured it out yet?"

"Don't have a clue," Kaden said.

"It's Xanadu spelled backward," Yo-Yo reported.

"Still clueless," Kaden said.

"I read about Xanadu the night I learned about zoysia

grass. When I grabbed the encyclopedia. Remember?"

"How could I forget?" Kaden said. "You jumped off the couch so fast to grab the book, Gram and I thought you were having some sort of conniption fit. So, what's Xanadu?"

"I'm surprised you don't know. Xanadu was an underground kingdom in a poem called 'Kubla Khan.' I didn't know about Kubla the crow when I read about Xanadu that night, but I picked the name for the sign in Kubla's honor."

As if he understood what Yo-Yo said, Kubla hopped down from his perch on the window frame and landed grasping the top edge of the board. He peered over at the dark letters as if reading them. Both boys laughed.

"I think he likes it," Kaden said. "But why spell it backward? And what about the 'X'? Shouldn't it be a 'Z'?"

"Xanadu is spelled with an 'X'; it just sounds like a 'Z.' And this place isn't exactly underground. It's the total opposite. So if Xanadu is the name for an underground kingdom, the opposite, Udanax, should be for an aboveground kingdom."

"Way aboveground," Kaden agreed. "You're right, it's perfect."

"So, here you go." Yo-Yo reached into his backpack, pulled out a hammer and nail, and handed them to Kaden. As Kaden nailed the sign above the metal chest, Yo-Yo pulled two cans of soda out of his backpack. The cold cans were sweating in the heat. He opened them, handed one to Kaden, and held his up in the air.

"We hereby christen this tower Udanax," Yo-Yo said, touching his can to the sign.

"The Aboveground Kingdom of Kubla," Kaden added. He, too, touched his can to the sign. The two boys chinked their cans together, took big swigs, and then burped as loudly as they could before sitting back down.

"Okay, what's that?" Kaden asked, pointing to a bright blue and yellow plastic tube sticking out of Yo-Yo's backpack.

"It's a periscope. You'll be able to see if your dad comes here again without him spotting you."

Kaden took the elongated S-shaped tube and looked inside one end. There were some angled mirrors. Then, holding it so that end was above the window, he looked through the other end. Without standing up, Kaden could see the log barricade. He moved the periscope around and saw the base of the tower. Moving it again, he saw the tree limb Kubla frequently sat on, then the woods and the clear blue sky that didn't offer a single shady cloud.

"Wicked!" he said. "But if Dad showed up, wouldn't he see this bright thing moving around up here?"

"That's why I brought this." Yo-Yo pulled out a roll of duct tape and wrapped some around the bright yellow end of the periscope. "Now it's camouflaged. If you keep it next to a window frame and move it slowly, I don't think you could see it from down there."

"We'll check it out when we leave," Kaden said. "You can stay up here until I get down and I'll see if I can spot it."

They went through the other items, picking them up one at a time.

"Camera," Yo-Yo announced, "so you can have a picture of your dad." Kaden hadn't told Yo-Yo about the photo album. But the photo of his dad holding him was at least nine years old. *It would be nice to have a current picture*, Kaden thought.

"It's only got a couple more shots on it," Yo-Yo said. "It's left over from music camp this summer. My mom gave me a throwaway, afraid I'd break or lose her digital camera."

"Baby wipes for you." Kaden laughed, rolling the container toward Yo-Yo. "And sunflower seeds for Kubla."

"You never know when you might need a flashlight," Yo-Yo said.

"A unique flashlight," Kaden added. "Is that what the batteries are for?"

"No, for the CD player. I can't find the electric cord that came with it but I'll keep looking. The batteries don't last very long."

"There's no electricity out here," Kaden said.

"I know, but you can take it home and listen there, too. It won't be heard through the intercom, not with the earbuds. So you can listen to stuff besides Gram's records," Yo-Yo said, holding up several CDs.

Kaden reached over and picked up the last thing, the cell phone. "This doesn't work," he said. "I tried to call you on it already."

"I know. It's an old one and we no longer go with that server," Yo-Yo answered. "But they say you can call 911 on any cell phone no matter whether you're hooked up to a plan or not. I threw it in, in case you ever need it."

"Do you think I will?"

"I don't know, but he has been in prison, and even though he's your dad, you don't know what he's really like or anything, do you? I've seen these cop shows on TV and—"

"You're right," Kaden interrupted him, "it's probably a good idea, just in case."

The boys had gone through all the items. Yo-Yo put a CD into the player, popped the earbuds in, leaned back into the corner, and closed his eyes.

Kaden stood up and leaned his elbows on a window frame. With a blur of flapping wings, Kubla landed on Kaden's head. A matchstick was in his beak. Without seeming to even be aware of the bird, Kaden took the matchstick and dropped it over the side of the tower.

Kubla caught it and returned. Kaden absently tossed the matchstick out again and looked down at Yo-Yo.

"Are you awake?" he asked. Yo-Yo said nothing. He was sound asleep. Kaden dropped the matchstick a third time. This time Kubla ignored the matchstick as it dropped toward the ground. Instead, the bird suddenly flew off toward the road, screeching his warning caw over and over, shattering the calm hum of insects.

Kaden was surprised. He hadn't heard a car. He ducked out of sight. Quietly picking up the periscope, he poked it slowly upward and looked through it. He saw no vehicles parked near the barricade. But what he did see made his heart instantly begin racing. Standing just behind the barricade stood his dad holding a long stick.

Kubla dove at Dad as he stepped over the barricade. Dad waved the stick and the crow veered off out of reach. He flew to his favorite branch, still cawing raucously as Dad walked toward the tower. Worried Dad would look up, Kaden pulled the periscope from the window. He wondered why his dad was at the tower. *Maybe he's leaving something for me again*, Kaden thought, but he hadn't seen anything in his hands except the stick.

Kubla squawked harshly a few more times, then quieted.

Kaden sat out of sight, his heart still pounding. *I wonder what he's doing*, he thought. Slowly, he poked the periscope up to the window again. He saw Kubla on his tree limb, but adjusting the periscope, he could not see his dad. He crawled quietly toward the open trapdoor in the floor and put the periscope out the opening just a little. Layers of stairs, alternating with metal grate landings, zigzagged down until they reached the last landing, twenty feet above the ground. Under the landing stood Dad, staring at the ground where the last set of stairs should have ended.

Dad dropped the stick, bent over, and picked something up. As he looked at what he held, Kubla suddenly came shrieking from the tree, flying straight toward him. His wild black wings fluttered around Dad's arm, and then the bird veered off. Kubla darted up, through the crisscross of steel beams, then circled around the flights of stairs to the top, as if climbing a spiral staircase. Kaden pulled the periscope in from the hole just as Kubla flew through it. He landed on Kaden's head, his black feet pricking Kaden's scalp as they grabbed his hair for balance. Kubla made several turning jumps until the bird and Kaden faced the same direction. Then Kubla bent over Kaden's forehead holding a matchstick he had taken from Dad's hand.

"Kaden!" a voice yelled out suddenly from below. "Kaden,

are you up there?"

Kaden froze, every muscle tight and rigid.

"I know you're here. Your grandmother said you were!" Dad yelled up again. Kubla, still holding the matchstick, jumped up to the window and looked intently below. The matchstick dropped to the ground as the bird gave several brassy caws.

Kaden glanced at Yo-Yo. He was still sleeping. Thursday night, Kaden swore he wouldn't hide from Dad, but he didn't want to meet him now. Not with Yo-Yo there. Kaden didn't move.

"Have it your way."

Kaden didn't hear another word. Finally Kubla left his watch post at the window. He hopped over to Kaden's shoulder, cooing and gurgling in Kaden's ear and pulling at his earlobe. Kaden inched the periscope past the edge of the hole in the floor and peered down. Dad was gone. He quietly moved it over to the window and scanned all around. Nothing.

CHAPTER TWENTY-ONE

READY

Kaden waited for a while to make sure Dad was gone, took a quick peek out the window, then gave Yo-Yo a shake.

"Dad was here again. You slept through it," Kaden said.

"What?" Yo-Yo said. He took out the earbuds and a thin trickle of music could be heard.

"My dad. He was here. Just now," Kaden repeated.

"Really? Did you talk to him?"

"No. I wasn't expecting him to come here and I didn't know what to do."

Yo-Yo stood up and looked out the window through the binoculars.

"I don't see his truck."

"He didn't drive in. He walked."

"Are you sure it was your dad?"

"Yeah. He called my name. And I recognized him from the other night."

"The other night?"

"Yeah. That's what I wanted to tell you about. Dad was at the cabins Thursday night when Gram was at the board meeting."

"Wow! So you've finally met him."

"No. He was in Cabin Five and didn't know I was home. It's not that I don't want to meet him, but every time I see him, I freeze. I'm just afraid of meeting him."

"Why?"

"I don't know. I was all ready to meet him and then Gram said he wasn't ready to meet me, and now I'm even more nervous about it. I think he is, too. I told you he left me the backpack. Well, he left a ball and glove, too, and Thursday, a photo album with pictures of him and me when I was a baby. It's like he wants to meet me, but . . ."

"Well, if he was here, he must be ready to meet you now."

"Yeah, but I'm not sure I'm ready."

"It's not too much different than standing up to Luke. You just have to act confident, even if you're not."

"I guess."

Yo-Yo looked at his watch. It was past five. "We'd better get going. My mom's going to be picking me up soon."

Kaden took the binoculars from Yo-Yo, put them in the chest, and closed the lid. But Yo-Yo opened it back up. He reached inside and pulled out the cell phone. "Maybe you should take this with you. You know, just in case."

Kaden took the phone and stood there looking at it in his hand. Then he shook his head and put the phone back in the chest.

"No, I won't need it," he said, and they headed down the stairs.

Kaden returned the rope with its rock to its hiding spot, and as he walked back under the tower, he picked up the stick his dad had dropped.

"Is it the one from the muddy spot?" Yo-Yo asked.

"Yeah," Kaden answered, but let the stick fall back to the ground. "No point in putting it back. It won't tell me anything if he walks in."

"You could set up a trip wire booby trap. I've seen them on TV. You're walking along and all of a sudden a rope goes around your ankle and before you know it you're hanging upside down from a tree."

Kaden said nothing but led the way down the path and over the barricade. As they walked down the road, Yo-Yo kept up with a stream of possibilities.

"Maybe you could dig a hole and put rattlesnakes in it and then cover it all up with branches. Or set up some invisible laser beams and if someone steps through them, they set off an alarm."

"You watch too much TV," Kaden said.

"Yeah, well, somebody has to." Yo-Yo grinned.

The two boys reached the back of the junk cabin, crept along the far side, and peeked around.

The white pickup was in front of Cabin Five. Mrs. Strokowski's SUV was in front of Gram's cabin and Emmett's truck was behind the SUV. Emmett was talking with Mrs. Strokowski through the car window. Gram was nowhere in sight. Neither was Dad.

"I'll stay if you want me to," Yo-Yo whispered.

"Thanks," Kaden said, "but I have to do this alone."

Yo-Yo and Kaden walked around the front of Cabin One and headed toward the SUV.

"She came out on the porch and said she had company, so I told her I'd just wait in the car," Mrs. Strokowski was telling Emmett as the boys walked up.

Kaden stood by Emmett, purposely keeping his back to Gram's cabin. Yo-Yo climbed in his mom's car, and as the SUV drove out of the circle drive, he opened the window and yelled out, "Good luck. See you Monday!"

But Kaden hardly heard. He stood there wondering if Dad was inside watching him.

Emmett turned to Kaden. "You know your dad is in there," he said quietly.

"Yeah, I know," Kaden said. He had been thinking about his dad but suddenly he wondered about Emmett. Emmett usually walked up to the cabins. This time he had driven. "Why are you here? Did Gram call you? Is something wrong?"

"No, I got here just a second before you did. Mrs. Strokowski called me to find out where you and Yo-Yo were. I think she's a little intimidated by your grandmother. So I thought I'd better come up. I didn't know your dad was here until I got here."

At the word "dad," Kaden tightened up again. Emmett took his hand for just a second and gave it a big squeeze. "You'll be all right."

"I know," Kaden said. He took a big breath and let it out slowly. "I'm ready."

CHAPTER TWENTY-TWO

THE MEETING

When Kaden and Emmett came in, Gram was on the couch and Dad was sitting in the easy chair. The chair Gram usually sat in. Dad watched them enter but he didn't get up.

"Howdy, Dennis," Emmett spoke first. His voice wasn't friendly, but it wasn't unfriendly either. Kaden noticed Emmett didn't step up to Dad or put out his hand.

"Emmett," Dad said, "been a long time." His voice wasn't overly friendly either, nor did he put out his hand.

Gram had not said a word, but now she spoke up. "Dennis, I taught you to stand when an elder enters the room. And take your hat off in the house."

"Yes, ma'am," Dad said in a sarcastic tone. He removed

his hat and slowly stood up. He gave Emmett a look that reminded Kaden of the looks he got from Luke.

Saying no more to Emmett, Dad turned to Kaden and with a much more pleasant voice said, "And you must be Kaden."

"Yes, sir," Kaden said.

"What's this sir stuff?" Dad said curtly. Kaden looked at the floor.

"The boy's been raised to be polite to strangers," Emmett said. His tone had not sweetened.

"Strangers, bull," Dad said. He turned to Kaden, his voice sweet again, but the tone of voice didn't match his words. "I'm not a stranger, son. I'm your dad. I know you already know that. I also know you saw me at the tower and didn't answer me."

This wasn't what Kaden imagined meeting his dad would be like. For years, he had imagined his dad running and picking him up, swinging him around and around, saying how much he missed him. For years, Kaden thought he knew what it would be like when Dad got out of prison. And until the last letter arrived three weeks ago, Kaden had looked forward to that day. Now Kaden didn't know what to say. He stood there, staring at the floor.

Gram stood up, taking Kaden off the hook. "We've all

been reunited now, so enough. Let's have dinner."

Emmett turned to leave but before he got the screen door opened, Gram said, "Emmett, you're staying. Kaden, go wash up."

Kaden rushed out the door, relieved to have a chance to get away. When he got in his cabin, he looked under his mattress. The photo album was still there. He looked at the picture again. In it Dad was smiling. Dad looked like he liked him. *Maybe Dad is just as nervous about our reintroduction as I am*, he thought.

Kaden could hear Gram through the intercom telling Emmett and Dad to behave themselves, that they were acting like a couple of strutting roosters. He heard the porch door slam shut and through his open window he heard the creak of the glider. He wished he could see who was sitting on the porch.

Through the intercom came the sound of pots and pans. That would be Gram. At the same time, there was the sound of the silverware drawer being opened and the chink of knives and forks. Someone was helping Gram. It could be either Emmett or Dad. Nobody said a word, so he couldn't tell which, but he knew there was only one person on the porch. He wished he had Yo-Yo's periscope.

Keeping his ears tuned, hoping to hear voices over the

intercom, Kaden washed his hands and face and changed out of his sweaty T-shirt. He paused at his desk but heard only sounds of dinner being prepared. *I've got to come out sometime*, he told himself. Hoping it was Emmett on the porch, he stepped out. It wasn't Emmett. It was Dad.

"Come on over here and sit down," Dad said. His voice no longer sounded sarcastic. "We can get to know each other a little before dinner. Did you find the presents I gave you?"

"Yes, thank you," Kaden said politely, but as he sat on the porch steps, anger started rising up in him. He could feel his body tense up thinking about why his father was giving him presents now. He never had before, at least not that he could remember. For eight years, he had never gotten anything from his father, not a letter, not a card, certainly not a present. All letters that came from Chapston City State Correctional Center had been addressed to Gram. Since Gram never let Kaden read any of them, he didn't know what they said, but no letters ever showed up around his birthday. Christmas cards arrived every year but they too were addressed to Gram, and Dad never wrote anything in them. He just signed them and they were always signed Dennis, not Dad. Kaden often wondered whether his father even remembered he lived with Gram. Or if his father even remembered he existed. And now he wondered if the stranger called Dad, who was sitting there in the glider as if he'd been there all along, thought the recent gifts would make up for the past.

"Why didn't you ever write me?" Kaden asked, not looking at his father.

Kaden said nothing more. Dad was silent also. Kaden could feel his father's eyes looking at him. Finally, Dad broke the silence.

"I know I haven't been a father to you and you have a right to be angry," he said. "I was wrong and I want to make it up to you now."

Kaden sat there. He didn't know what to think. He thought it'd be simple to just forgive and forget but it wasn't. Kaden felt like shouting. At the same time, he wanted to cry. He also wanted Gram or Emmett, or even the stranger called Dad, to give him a hug. But none of that happened. He stood up, not saying a word, and walked back to his cabin. Without turning on the light, he lay down on his bed.

Kaden heard Gram's screen door open and close again. Then Dad's voice came through the intercom.

"What's his problem?" Dad said. "He won't even talk to me."

"You can't come waltzing into his life and expect him to be your long-lost buddy," Gram answered.

"A boy should respect his father," Dad said. "I was trying to be nice and he got up and walked away."

"You've done nothing for him to respect," Emmett said. "You're just a stranger to him and you can't deny it."

Kaden knew Gram and Emmett were both aware he would be listening. It surprised him because they usually turned off the intercom or went to the garden to talk. Kaden also wondered if Dad knew about the intercom system. It didn't sound like he did.

"I'm not a stranger," Dad stated forcefully. "I know all sorts of stuff about him. I had all his pictures taped to my wall. I know he likes to fish, he helps you in the garden and Emmett in the shop, he goes to the fire tower. He does all the stuff I used to do when we came here in the summer."

"You only know that because I told you about him and sent you his school pictures," Gram stated. "What did you ever send him?"

"I wasn't exactly some place where I could go shopping, you know."

"I don't mean things. You could have written to him," Gram said. "You may think you know him, but you don't. And he knows nothing about you."

"I sent letters every so often," Dad said.

"You sent *me* letters," Gram said, "not Kaden. And they were all about you. Complaining about the food, complaining about the work, complaining about everything. You never once asked about your son."

"I figured you'd tell him about me," Dad said.

"Well, you figured wrong," Gram said. "It was your decision to stay out of his life. If you want to be his father now, you'll have to prove yourself to Kaden, not the other way around. Now eat some dinner and lock the door behind you. I'm going to bed."

"I'm not hungry," Dad retorted.

Kaden heard Gram's bedroom door close. At the same time, the screen door opened and slammed shut. He wondered why Gram said to lock the door. Gram never locked the door. Footsteps went down the porch steps and turned toward Kaden's cabin. Kaden climbed out of bed, quietly shut the solid wooden door, and locked it. Back on the bed, he heard the footsteps stop halfway between Cabins Three and Two. Then he heard them again. But this time, they turned away from Kaden's cabin and walked the other direction. Kaden gave a sigh of relief. If that was Dad, he was glad he didn't come talk with him.

Kaden lay on his bed, listening. Quiet sounds of dishes clinking together, the refrigerator opening and closing, and water running and then stopping came through the intercom. Then, surprisingly, the calming notes of a cello and Gram's heavy wooden front door clicking shut. Through his open window Kaden heard the sound of Gram's screen door closing. The creak of the porch stairs and footsteps across the gravel to his cabin. The sound of something being set outside Kaden's closed door. Footsteps retreating across gravel. Emmett's truck door squeaking open, slamming shut. The motor turning on and the truck pulling out of the drive.

Kaden got out of bed and opened his door. There was a plate of food and a glass of milk.

Sunday, September 11

CHAPTER TWENTY-THREE

LIKE A NORMAL FAMILY

When Kaden awoke, he listened attentively to the sounds both over the intercom and through the window. It sounded like any Sunday morning. Gram was in the kitchen. Only the sound of birds came from outside. Kaden opened the cabin door. He cautiously stuck his head out. Nobody was in sight. But the white truck was still in front of Cabin Five.

Kaden went into the kitchen and gave Gram a hug.

"You stink. Go take a shower while I fix breakfast," Gram said, but hugged him back.

Kaden opened the screen door, looked both ways, and hurried to his cabin to get some clean clothes. Then he rushed to Cabin Four. After his shower, Kaden peeked his head out the door. *Still clear*, he thought, and laughed to himself. He had told Yo-Yo he watched too much TV. Kaden hardly watched any TV at all yet he felt like he was in a spy show.

"I haven't heard you practice that trumpet once," Gram said as they finished their oatmeal. She had insisted on eating on the porch just like they always did. Kaden was glad Gram seemed back to her normal self. "If you get kicked out of band for not practicing, I'll have to make another trip to that school to get rid of the other two days of study hall."

"I don't think Mr. Price could survive that," Kaden said, grinning. Gram actually grinned back.

Kaden got his trumpet and came back to sit on the porch steps. He leaned against the railing, his back to Cabins Four and Five. Squeaks and squeals poured out of the brass instrument but every once in a while he hit a pure tone.

"That was a good one," Gram stated. "Try it again."

Kaden kept trying, hitting more and more clear notes. He figured out if he held his mouth slightly differently the note would change pitches. After about five minutes, Kaden tried pushing each of the valves down as he blew. He had all but forgotten about his dad and didn't hear him walking up the drive until he spoke.

"You sure make a racket first thing in the morning," Dad stated. Kaden turned around. Dad was smiling as he walked up to the porch holding a set of clothes. "I'm going to take a shower before breakfast."

"Breakfast is over," Gram said, "but there's coffee on the stove. And the shower is in Cabin Four now. We don't use the shower in my cabin anymore. It's a closet now."

Dad put his clothes on one of the metal chairs, went into Gram's cabin, and returned with a piece of toast and a cup of coffee.

"So, you're playing the trumpet," he said as he sat down on the top step opposite Kaden.

"Just starting," Kaden said. He picked a tall piece of grass growing beside the steps and twirled it between his fingers. All the tension of the night before seemed to have melted in the early morning sun.

"I didn't play in band," Dad said. "Mom, I mean your grandmother—"

Gram interrupted him. "He calls me Gram," she said. "And I don't have time to sit around talking. I've got a garden to tend." Gram got up and walked around to the back of the cabin, leaving Kaden with his father.

"She's always a little gruff in the morning," Kaden said.

"I know. And in the afternoon, too—unless she's changed," Dad said, laughing.

"And don't forget the evening," Kaden added, smiling.

"Anyway," Dad continued, "your Gram wanted me to be in band, but I didn't want to wear those band uniforms. They looked ridiculous. But I'm glad you've decided to play an instrument."

Kaden thought about what Luke had said. At least Dad didn't say he was a loser.

"I don't have a uniform yet," Kaden said. "They're getting new ones soon."

"So do you play sports?" Dad asked.

"Just in PE," Kaden said.

"Are you going to try out for a school team?"

"Not this year. You have to be in seventh grade."

"What grade are you in?"

"Sixth," Kaden answered. Gram was right. Dad didn't really know anything about him. But he was trying to, and Kaden relaxed a little.

"Oh," Dad said. "Well, I've been asking all the questions. Do you have any questions about me?"

Kaden had tons of questions. He wanted to know everything but he didn't know where to start. "Not really," he said, shrugging.

"Well, I didn't play on a school team either," Dad said. "Mom was upset about that, too, but me and my friends just kind of hung out, you know?"

Kaden didn't say anything. He didn't figure it was really a question. But it sounded like Gram had been a lot different with Dad. She wanted Dad to do a lot of things, like be in band and play sports. But she hardly let Kaden do anything. Dad sat there, waiting for Kaden to say something, but Kaden just stared at the piece of grass he was twirling. Finally, Dad sighed.

"How about playing a little catch?" Dad asked. "Go get that glove and ball. I'm sure you found them on your bed. I can take a shower later."

Kaden was relieved. Throwing a ball around was better than having to talk. He took his trumpet into his cabin and came out holding the new glove and ball in his right hand. An old mitt was on his left hand.

"Where'd you get that old thing?" Dad said.

"It was Emmett's. He gave it to me for my seventh birthday." Kaden held the new mitt and ball to his dad.

"Well, take it off and use the one I gave you."

"No, you can use it. I'll use Emmett's," Kaden said, still holding the new glove out to his dad.

"Whatever," Dad said. He roughly grabbed the new glove, put it on, and tossed the ball into it a few times as he walked across the crescent-shaped lawn. Kaden walked to the opposite end.

"Ready?" Dad asked. His voice had lost its friendliness.

"Ready," Kaden answered.

Dad threw the ball, hard and fast. It landed in Kaden's glove with a loud smack. Kaden's hand stung but he didn't say a word. He tried to throw it back hard but didn't have the force behind it. Dad caught it and threw another fastball. Kaden was good at catch. He and Emmett threw the ball back and forth all the time. Emmett threw some zingers, too, but it wasn't the same and Kaden knew it.

Kaden kept catching whatever was thrown at him. He knew his dad was mad at him for not using the new glove but it wasn't that he didn't want to use it. Kaden just didn't want Dad to use Emmett's. It had been a special present.

That's stupid, he told himself as he threw the ball back. *Dad's been nice all morning and he did get a new glove for me. He's trying but I'm the one being a jerk.* Kaden caught another ball and called out, "Let me try that glove for a while."

Dad smiled as they switched gloves. He didn't throw any more zingers but started acting more like the way Emmett acted when they played catch, saying, "Here's a pop fly," and "Let's practice some grounders."

When they tired of playing, the two walked back to the porch.

"You're pretty good," Dad said. "Ever thought of signing up for Little League?"

"Too late now," Kaden said. "They only play in the summer."

"Well, you should try out at school when you get to seventh grade," Dad said, sitting down on the porch steps. "So what do you want to do now?"

"I don't know," Kaden said. "I have some homework. Gram will ask about it at lunch."

"Well, then get to it. I'll take a shower and we'll watch a game after lunch."

"Can't," Kaden said. "We don't have a TV."

"Really? I guess I didn't notice," Dad said.

"If there's anything we really want to watch, we go down to Emmett's," Kaden explained.

"So how do you know what's going on in the world? Your Gram doesn't even get a newspaper. I found that out yesterday," Dad said.

"We read the paper at Emmett's, too. Or he brings them up here. Sometimes, it's a few days old but Gram says if there's ever any news that's going to directly affect her life, she's sure someone will drive up here and tell her. Otherwise, hearing what happens can wait a few days," Kaden said. "Did you have a TV and newspapers when you were a kid?"

"Of course," Dad said.

"Even here, in the summer?"

"The newspaper was delivered here every morning," Dad said, "but we didn't have TV up here. That was one of the reasons I didn't want to come anymore. I was pretty bored around here."

"It's not so bad. I do a bunch of stuff with Emmett and I like hanging out at the tower."

"So what else do you have to go to Emmett for?" Dad said. "Sounds like the old man's gotten in pretty tight around here. But he always was butting into things that weren't his business. I wouldn't trust that old fool too much if I were you."

"Emmett's always been good to us," Kaden said defensively, the tension instantly back in play.

"I shouldn't have said that to you," Dad said. His voice was back to friendly. "I'm sure he's helped out a lot. But I'm here now and can take charge. Go tell Gram we're going into town."

"Town? Nothing's open on Sunday except Pillie's," Kaden said, "and I really don't—"

"We're not going to Promise," Dad interrupted. "We're going to Chapston City."

Kaden was relieved. He didn't want to show up with Dad at Pillie's.

They were gone the rest of the day. When they pulled back into the circle drive, Gram was inside fixing dinner. Dad backed the truck up to the porch steps and opened the cargo carrier. There were only two things in it. An old sleeping bag and a large box.

Kaden held the screen door open as Dad hauled the box into the living room. Gram stood in the kitchen, her hands on her hips.

"Who said I wanted a TV?" Gram stated, seeing the words printed on the box.

"Nobody. I wanted it," Dad said.

"And just where do you think you're going to put it?"

"It will hang over there on the wall. When you want to watch it, you can just pull it out in front of the window and push it back when you're done. If we angle it right, we can watch while we eat."

"We're not watching TV while we eat," Gram stated.

"We did when I was a kid."

"Well, we don't anymore."

"You've certainly changed. What's gotten into you?"

"I'm just not repeating history," Gram said, but she didn't say the TV had to go.

Dad barely had the TV out of the box before dinner was ready. As they sat down to eat, Gram brought it up again.

"So I take it you've gotten a job during the last two weeks," she said.

"No, I've been looking," Dad said. "In Chapston City."

"Then where'd you get the money?" she asked.

"Where my money comes from is my business," Dad said. "And I should be able to buy a gift for the family without getting the third degree."

Gram didn't say any more. After supper, she sat on the porch. Kaden did the dishes and then helped his dad mount the TV to the wall. It took all evening but as soon as they turned it on, Gram came back in the cabin. With Gram in her chair, Dad stretched out on the couch, and Kaden sprawled on the floor, the three watched the ten o'clock news. *Just like a normal family*, Kaden thought.

When the news was over, Gram picked up the remote and turned off the TV.

"I don't think there was anything I heard I really needed to know," she said, "but I do know it cost you a lot for me to hear it. Now, it's way past bedtime for Kaden and me. Turn off the lights and lock the door behind you." Gram took the remote back in the bedroom with her.

Saying good night, Dad went to Cabin Five, and locking

Gram's door behind him, Kaden went to his cabin. He closed his wooden door and locked it, too. Climbing into bed, he heard Gram's bedroom door open and footsteps cross the living room.

"Did everything go okay today with your father?" Kaden heard through the intercom. "I was worried about him taking off with you like that."

"Everything went just fine, Gram. We had a good time."

"Good. I'll see you in the morning."

Kaden didn't know why Gram would be worried. He lay in bed until he heard Gram go back in her room. Then he quietly got up, unlocked the door and opened it wide, letting the evening air come through the screen door as it usually did.

Monday, September 12

CHAPTER TWENTY-FOUR

TOWN CRIER

"Whose truck is that and what's it doing in the middle of the driveway?" Doris asked when Kaden stepped onto the bus. "I had to drive on your lawn to get around it."

Kaden hesitated but knew he couldn't hide the fact a white pickup sat in front of Cabin Five.

"It's my dad's," Kaden said.

"He's home?" Doris seemed genuinely surprised.

"Yeah, we didn't think about the bus. This afternoon, I'll tell him to keep it parked out of the way."

"When did he get here?" Doris asked. "I can't believe I haven't heard a word about this, not one word."

Doris heard all the gossip in Promise and spread most of

it. They had kept quiet about Dad getting out of prison but Kaden knew that the whole town would learn about it as soon as Doris dropped off the elementary students. Doris wouldn't be able to get over to Pillie's fast enough. Pillie always had a crowd for morning coffee and Doris would have a good-size audience.

"Saturday," Kaden told her.

"So he's back in Cabin Five, huh? Is he staying long? Does he have a job? How did he look? I haven't seen him since your grandpa died. And what was in that big box in the back of his truck?"

Doris kept up a steady stream of questions and comments. Kaden answered them, knowing there was no point in trying to hold things back, but was glad Emmett didn't live far away.

"Do you know Dennis is at the cabins?" Doris asked Emmett as he held open the kitchen door.

"Yeah, I saw him Saturday. Go on in. I need Kaden to help me carry some things in from the garden."

Kaden followed Emmett around to back of the shop. Two bushel baskets of corn, beans, cucumbers, peppers, and tomatoes were waiting but Kaden knew Emmett was using the garden to talk to him in private.

"So how was yesterday?" Emmett asked. "I figured it would be best if I stayed away."

"Long," Kaden said. "Started out kind of rough but not like Saturday night. Just uncomfortable. But it got better as the day went on." Kaden didn't tell Emmett what Dad said about him. Or about the way Dad threw the fastballs at him.

"Good," said Emmett. "It will take some time to get adjusted. You know, people can change if they want to. We'll see how it all works out. And your Gram? How's she holding up?"

"She's okay. I was surprised she didn't get too upset at the TV."

"TV?" Emmett asked.

"Yeah. Dad and I went to Chapston City and bought one. Gram even watched the news on it."

"See, didn't I just tell you? People can change." Emmett laughed. They each picked up a basket of vegetables and walked back to the house.

"Are you going to make pickles?" Doris asked. "I love your spicy hot ones."

"Not enough time. I have all that wood to split back there." Emmett sold firewood to half of Promise and gave it away to the other half.

"This early?" Kaden asked. "It's only September. We haven't even had a frost yet."

"I know, but I told Clarence I'd have three cords for him

by the middle of the month and I don't work as fast as I used to. These old bones get pretty stiff leaning over and picking up logs."

"You shouldn't use that splitter by yourself," Doris said. "It's dangerous. You could chop your arm off with that thing."

Kaden had seen the splitting machine in Emmett's shop and Emmett had shown him how it used hydraulic pressure to cram a log into a wedge to split it. He knew one slip and the wedge could split an arm in two.

"Doris is right," Kaden now told Emmett. "You've always said it was safest to have two people running it."

"Well, if you're going to side with Doris, maybe you and Yo-Yo could help me with it this weekend?"

"Sure, if the pay's right," Kaden said, grinning. "How about another Jumbo Lightning Moo-Cream?"

At school, Yo-Yo was waiting impatiently in Ms. Ales's room.

"So, what was he like? I've been dying to know. You guys really have to get a phone. Did he have prison tats? Big muscles and stuff? You know, they do a lot of weight lifting in prison."

Once Yo-Yo started, he couldn't stop. He asked as many

questions as Doris but his were entirely different.

"And what about scars? Any scars? You know, from knife fights? Every prison show I've ever seen has a knife fight. They sharpen a spoon and hide it in the laundry and then someone buys it with cigarettes and hides it under their mattress, just waiting for the right opportunity. Does your dad smoke cigarettes?"

"Enough already. If you'd shut up for a minute, I'd have a chance to answer." Yo-Yo slapped his hand over his mouth and Kaden continued.

"Yes, he's very muscular and he has a tattoo—"

"What's it look like?" Yo-Yo interrupted.

"A band of barbed wire around his left bicep. But I didn't see any scars. He didn't smoke any cigarettes and I didn't see any in his truck either."

"You were in his truck? What did you do, sneak out in the middle of the night and search through it? What's in the cargo carrier? I should have told you to take the flashlight home instead of leaving it at the tower."

"No, I didn't search his truck. We went to Chapston City in it. And the only thing in the cargo carrier is an old sleeping bag."

"You went to Chapston City?"

"Yeah, he bought us a TV."

"Awesome! How big is it? Is it a wide-screen? High-def? Does it have surround sound? What about 3-D?"

"It's not very big," Kaden said, laughing. "A big one wouldn't fit in Gram's cabin. There's no cable or satellite out there, so we only get three stations."

First bell rang and voices could be heard coming down the hall.

"No more right now. We'll talk later when we can be alone," Kaden said. "Oh, and before I forget, Emmett wants you and me to help him split wood Saturday. Think your mom will let you?"

"Split wood?" Yo-Yo asked. "Sweet! I've never used an ax before. You think I'll be able to lift it? I don't exactly have a Paul Bunyan body, you know."

"You don't use an ax; you use a log splitter. It runs on gas," Kaden explained. "We'll help lift logs onto it and stack the split wood on Emmett's trailer. After we deliver it to Clarence, Emmett will take us to Pillie's."

"I thought I told you to stay away from Pillie's." Luke had come up behind them. He had evidently made up with Elana, because she was right beside him.

"Luke, you can't say who can come in my parents' restaurant," Elana said. "I've talked my mom into letting you back in but I'm warning you, if she hears you're threatening people, she'll kick you out again."

"You don't need to warn me; you need to warn your mom. Kaden's dad is out. She better keep a gun handy if she doesn't want to be robbed."

Kaden knew the news would travel fast but he couldn't believe it would get to the school that quickly.

Elana rolled her eyes at Luke. "Why are you telling me that? I'm the one who told you." Then she turned to Kaden to explain. "The restaurant was swamped this morning so I was still there helping when Doris came charging in with the news about your dad."

"Well, with a con on the loose, you can't be too careful. Fresh out of prison, no job, and he's already shown up with a TV." Luke turned to Kaden. "How big was it, Kaden? Small enough to easily lift?"

Second bell rang. Ms. Ales walked in. Luke put his mouth up close to Kaden's ear. "I'm warning you, stay away from Pillie's," he whispered.

CHAPTER TWENTY-FIVE

SCHOOL BEAUTIFICATION

It was sixth-grade week for School Beautification Duty. After lunch, the cooks handed the girls wet rags to wipe ketchup and spilled milk off the tables. Then some of the boys moved the tables into the storage room. Other students swept up the mess of crumbs, bits of food, and straw wrappers left on the floor. Everyone was busy working except Luke. Luke leaned against the wall by the door. Coach Dosser leaned against the wall next to him. Almost all evidence of a school lunch had been removed and the cafeteria had almost transformed back into a gym when Mr. Price came in. He glanced at Luke.

"My dad said I don't have to be a janitor around here," Luke instantly spoke up.

Mr. Price ignored Luke but took Coach Dosser aside. Then he walked over to Kaden and Yo-Yo.

"Come with me," he said.

Mr. Price led the way. A white truck was backed up to the back doors of the school, its bed filled with long boxes covered in clear plastic wrap. Kaden's first thought was it was his father, but then he saw Mr. Schmerz pulling one of the boxes toward him across the open tailgate. Already a bunch of new trowels, hoses, and other garden equipment was piled up inside the doors.

"Your grandmother said you two would know what to do with these," Mr. Price said, pointing to the boxes Mr. Schmerz was stacking inside. Stamped in big block letters across each box was ZOYSIA GRASS PLUGS / KEEP SHADED UNTIL PLANTED. One of the boxes had an envelope attached to the top.

"Yes, sir," Kaden said, giving Yo-Yo a glance. "We know all about zoysia grass, don't we, Yo-Yo?"

"Oh, yeah, tons," Yo-Yo said. "And I think we're going to find out even more, up close and personal."

"Good," Mr. Price said. "Then you're in charge. They're for the courtyard. You and the other sixth graders can get started planting them today during C.A.R.E. I'm sure that won't be nearly enough time but I can't have all the sixth graders out there all afternoon. So you two are dismissed from afternoon classes to work on it. If you can't get done today, we should be able to keep what's not planted alive until Wednesday."

The janitor came around the corner with a dolly. Mr. Price left. Kaden and Yo-Yo helped the janitor stack the boxes on the dolly. Only half of them fit. Taking the garden equipment, the boys followed the janitor back down the hall, through the library, and out into the courtyard. Coach Dosser was waiting there with the rest of the sixth graders.

"Gram was right," Yo-Yo said, looking around at the remnants of weedy gardens and sparse patches of grass scattered in the hardened dirt. "This place could do with a makeover."

Kaden removed the envelope from the top box and opened it. Yo-Yo looked over his shoulder at the papers inside. They were instructions on the planting and care of zoysia grass plugs. When the janitor came back with a second load of boxes, he reached in his pocket and handed Kaden a pocketknife.

"Price said you're in charge," the janitor told him. "You're going to need this to cut through that plastic."

Kaden must have looked surprised.

"I know all about school rules," the janitor said. "They're ridiculous. This is a tool, not a weapon, and I've got other

stuff to do. You can give it back to me at the end of the day."
The janitor left, leaving Kaden holding the pocketknife.

Kaden opened the knife, slit through the plastic wrap,
and opened one of the boxes. Inside were rows and rows
of little grass stubs, each in a tablespoon-size ball of damp
dirt. Yo-Yo counted. Four rows, twenty-five in each. Kaden
counted the boxes. Thirty.

"Do you realize how many zoysia grass plugs we're going
to have to plant?" Kaden said, closing the knife and slipping
it in his pocket.

"Yeah, but I've got a plan," Yo-Yo said, grabbing the directions. He put a trowel and a grass plug on the picnic table
near the library door and jumped up on the tabletop.

"Hey, listen up!" Yo-Yo yelled. Nobody paid any attention
to him. Like a teacher, Yo-Yo clapped his hands first slowly
two times, then quickly three times. The students immediately quieted and clapped back, two times slowly, three times
quickly. Even Luke spontaneously responded. Kaden was
glad Gram didn't see that. She would have said something
about students being trained like circus monkeys. But it
worked. Yo-Yo had their attention.

"My fellow sixth graders," Yo-Yo started, "we've been
given our mission. We are to beautify this courtyard by
planting a specimen of grass called zoysia." Yo-Yo held up the

grass plug. "Coach, you should be especially pleased to know this kind of grass is frequently used on golf courses. Once it takes hold, you should be able to set up a putting green in the middle of the courtyard."

The students started talking again, so Yo-Yo clapped his hands to get their attention back.

"First," Yo-Yo said, looking at the directions, "the ground must be watered thoroughly. Sarah-with-an-H, that will be your job. You can start right now while I'm talking. Get it wet, but not muddy." Kaden screwed the hose to the spigot and turned it on for Sarah. As she pulled the hose to the middle of the courtyard and started spraying, Yo-Yo held up a trowel.

"There are eight boys and we have eight trowels, so the boys will dig little holes."

"I'm not digging nothing," Luke called out. "And who said you could give orders, anyway?"

To Kaden's surprise, Coach Dosser came forward out of the shade. "Mr. Price said Kaden and Yo-Yo are in charge. Luke, you're digging. My orders."

Yo-Yo continued reading the directions aloud. "The holes need to be about three inches deep and six inches apart, in a chessboard pattern." He stopped and looked out at the students. "Sara-without-an-H, go to Mr. Herd's room and get eight rulers."

"I don't understand," Phillip called out.

"Of course you don't, Phillip," Luke scoffed. "It takes brains to play chess."

Yo-Yo ignored Luke. "Picture a chessboard, Phillip. Dig holes only on the black squares. The white squares are the six inches of dirt in between."

"Oh, I get it, the rows are staggered," Phillip said.

"Kind of like your brain," Luke said.

Kaden had had enough of Luke, and without even thinking, the words going through his mind came out of his mouth, loud and clear. "Shut up, Luke."

It startled Kaden that he actually said that, and it must have startled Luke, too. He looked at Kaden in surprise but before he could say anything, Elana spoke up.

"Yeah, Luke, be quiet," she said. But Luke had regained his composure.

"Has everyone forgotten we'd all be sitting nice and cool in study hall having a good time instead of out here planting grass in the hot sun if Kaden's grandma hadn't stuck her nose where it didn't belong?"

"I think she was right," Elana said. "The courtyard needs work."

"Me too," several of the other students chimed in. Kaden smiled to himself, surprised by how many had the courage to stand up against Luke.

"Well, do what you want," Luke said, "but I'm not going to be treated like a prisoner sentenced to hard labor." He stomped off and sat under a tree at the far end of the courtyard. A couple of other boys joined the mutiny.

"Get back up here," Coach called out. Luke didn't budge. Neither did the other boys.

"Extra laps in PE for those who don't participate," Coach said sternly. The other boys got up and joined the rest of the class but Luke stayed under the tree. Coach crossed his arms and took two steps forward. Luke got up and slowly started sauntering back.

"Okay, back to directions," Yo-Yo started up again. "The girls will be planters."

"I thought I was the waterer," Sarah said. As she spoke, she turned to look at Yo-Yo. The hose changed directions and water sprayed all over Luke.

"Hey, watch what you're doing," Luke snapped at Sarah. The whole class laughed.

"Sorry," Sarah said, but then started giggling. "Looks like you peed your pants."

The class laughed even harder. Yo-Yo let them laugh for a while before he clapped his hands again.

"Yes, Sarah, your job is to water the ground to soften it

up," Yo-Yo continued. "Watering Luke was a nice try but I don't think he softened up any."

Luke scowled. The class laughed again. Yo-Yo was on top of his game.

"Okay," Yo-Yo said. "Let's get to work."

Coach opened the library door. "Behave yourselves," he said. "I'll be watching from inside." Kaden could see through the window as Coach Dosser sat in the air-conditioned room, his feet up on a table.

Everyone worked diligently, talking and laughing as they dug and planted. Everyone but Luke. He had gone back to the shade of the tree. Kaden kept an eye on him but Luke seemed focused on Elana and Yo-Yo. They were digging and planting as a team. Elana pulled out a pair of earbuds, the cord running down to the pocket of her capris. She gave one earbud to Yo-Yo and put the other in her ear. As they worked closely side by side sharing the earbuds, Luke's scowl got bigger and bigger.

Kaden was about to give Yo-Yo the heads-up about Luke when Coach opened the door and stepped onto the patio.

"Five minutes 'til the bell rings," he announced. "Go wash up before your next class." Luke was the first one in the door.

As the rest of the class filed inside, Yo-Yo and Kaden put down their trowels, stood up, and stretched.

"Ten empty and two rows gone from the eleventh box. Barely a third," Yo-Yo groaned.

Kaden slid the half-empty box of plugs over to an area of dampened dirt and returned to his hands and knees.

"Next time," he told Yo-Yo, "be more selective about what you read aloud in front of Gram."

CHAPTER TWENTY-SIX

SHARING MUSIC

When the last student to come out the middle-school door stepped on the bus, Doris didn't pull forward.

"Where's Luke?" she called out.

No one knew where Luke was, and Doris was obviously irritated. She radioed in to the school office to report Luke missing, then pulled forward to the elementary door. The younger students boarded the bus but Doris stayed put. She waited until Luke had been located, not at school but at Pillie's. Doris was fifteen minutes off schedule and not too pleased.

As the bus let out the last student before heading up the hill out of town, Kaden moved up to the seat behind Doris.

"Could you stop at Emmett's?" he asked. "I want to let

him know Yo-Yo and I can help him split wood on Saturday. And you could use a little treat."

"Well, for just a second," Doris said as she swung the bus into Emmett's driveway.

"Yo-Yo made the wall," Emmett announced as Kaden and Doris entered the kitchen.

"You got the fishing pictures developed already?" Kaden asked. Emmett's old camera used real film and sometimes it was months before he took enough pictures to use up a whole roll.

"Right there," Emmett said, pointing to a photograph. Yo-Yo was holding up a not-very-big sunfish but a record-size smile stretched across his face. His hair was sopping and his wet shirt clung to his body. It was the first fish Yo-Yo ever caught. He was so excited when the fish tugged on the line, he fell off the log he was standing on, right into the water. But he landed the fish.

"Sweet! He'll love it when he sees it," Kaden told Emmett.

"Never seen a boy fall into the river as many times as that boy did," Emmett said, "but he always came up grinning. I took two. You can give one to Yo-Yo."

"You can give it to him yourself," Kaden said. "He'll be here with me Saturday to split wood."

"Good," said Emmett. "So, who wants pie and ice cream?"

It was more than an hour before Doris let Kaden off at the cabins. Gram sat on the couch with her feet up. The TV was on. She had a glass of iced tea in one hand and the remote in the other.

"Don't know why people are so enamored with televisions," she said, not even glancing at Kaden, who went straight to the refrigerator and put in half a pie. "Used to be good shows on TV, but there was nothing on all afternoon worth watching."

Gram turned off the TV and looked up as Kaden turned around.

"What happened to you?" she said. Kaden's face was streaked with sweat and dirt. His T-shirt had dirty hand marks down the front and his knees were covered with caked mud.

"Zoysia grass," was all he said. He had to explain it thoroughly to Doris and Emmett but Gram didn't need any more of an explanation.

"Oh, good. I was wondering if it got there," Gram said. "How much did you get planted?"

"One thousand, nine hundred and fifty-seven," Kaden said.

"All in fifty minutes?" Gram said. "I should have bought

a thousand more."

"No, you bought enough," Kaden said. Plopping down on a kitchen chair, he told her how he and Yo-Yo planted 907 by themselves.

"Don't worry," Gram said. "I'm not going to order any more. We'll see how these take first. Why don't you go take a shower?"

"That's exactly what I was planning," Kaden said. "Where's Dad?" The white truck was not in the driveway.

"He was gone most of the day. He has to meet with his parole officer every Monday and Wednesday," Gram said. "But when he came back this afternoon, we had a little disagreement."

"About what?"

"He wanted you to go with him to visit his friends and I told him you couldn't, not on a school night."

"He got mad about that?"

"That and my telling him I wasn't too keen on you hanging around with his friends. I told him I need to know where you are and who you're with," Gram said.

"I was at Emmett's," Kaden said. "I needed to tell him Yo-Yo can come help split wood Saturday."

"I knew where you were," Gram said, "or at least I assumed I knew."

"What if Dad had stopped at Emmett's for me?"

"I thought of that," Gram said, "but I trust you would have the good sense to say no on a school night. And to tell me where you were going." Gram paused and started chuckling. "Not to mention, I know Doris and her rules. Doris would insist she bring you to the proper destination. Your dad would be no match against Doris when it came to obeying her rules."

Kaden laughed with Gram, imagining Doris in a standoff with Dad. As he walked over to his cabin to get clean clothes, Kaden thought about what Yo-Yo would be saying if he had heard Gram. Yo-Yo would have Doris holding Kaden hostage in the bus with SWAT teams aiming guns at Dad's white pickup. Yo-Yo's influence had taken over and Kaden was in full TV-cop-show mode when he opened the screen door and stopped cold. Sitting on his bed was another gift. An MP3 player. A note was sitting beside it.

Got this from a friend. Thought you'd like to hear something besides that old stuff your grandma plays. —Dad

It kind of creeped Kaden out that when he least expected it, Dad had been there. In his room. In the tower. If Dad was going to give him gifts, he wished he would do it in person, face-to-face. *Maybe it's just hard for him to show his feelings*, Kaden thought. Kaden put the note under the mattress with the photo album. Then he picked up the MP3 player, put the earbuds in, and turned it on. It was already loaded with a ton of music. He listened as he grabbed his clothes and went to Cabin Four. When he got done with his shower, Gram was on the porch.

"What's that?" Gram asked, pointing to the cords coming from Kaden's pocket to his ears.

"It's an MP3 player," Kaden answered. "Dad left it on my bed."

"What's an MP3 player?" Gram asked.

"It plays music," Kaden said, pulling it out of his pocket and showing it to Gram. "Didn't Dad show it to you?"

"No, didn't say a word about it," Gram said. "How much does one of those cost?"

"I don't know, quite a bit," Kaden said, "but I don't think he paid anything. There was a note. He said he got it from a friend."

"Is that right?" Gram stated. "So how does it work?"

Kaden told Gram how music was downloaded onto it.

"Just no playing music while you're supposed to be studying," Gram said as she got up.

"Okay," Kaden said, following her into the cabin.

"Now put some music on the turntable so we can both listen," Gram said, pulling out an album from under the sink. Soon Gram was singing along about a big tough guy nobody messed around with. Kaden got Gram laughing as he drowned out the chorus, singing how you couldn't mess around with Gram either.

The rest of the evening felt good. Just Kaden and Gram. Back to normal. Except after dishes, Kaden turned on a TV and Gram watched, too.

Tuesday, September 13

CHAPTER TWENTY-SEVEN

FRAMED

When Kaden walked down the hall before first bell, Elana was standing by her locker. All its contents were dumped in a heap on the floor in front of it. Yo-Yo was sitting on the floor, searching through her backpack.

"What are you looking for?" Kaden asked.

"Elana's MP3," Yo-Yo answered.

Kaden instantly had a sickening feeling in the pit of his stomach but he didn't say a word.

"You sure you didn't leave it in Clary's class?" Yo-Yo asked.

"No way," Elana said. "I made sure it was out of sight before I stepped into Scary Clary's."

"I'm sure it's at Pillie's," Yo-Yo stated. "I've seen you wear it while you work."

"No, I've told you," Elana said, "Mom doesn't like me to listen if there are customers. I put it in my backpack after C.A.R.E. yesterday, and when I looked for it this morning, it wasn't there."

Kaden didn't want to ask but he knew he had to. "Could somebody have taken it at Pillie's?"

Elana didn't seem to notice the worried tone in Kaden's voice but Yo-Yo looked up at him.

"I don't think so," Elana said. "It was just me and Luke. And some man. I don't know who he was. I've never seen him before. Luke and I sat at the back table and the only time I wasn't near my backpack was when I brought our sundaes out. But Luke was right there with my backpack the whole time, so no one could have taken it."

"What about after you were done eating?" Kaden asked. "Did you leave the room?"

"Yeah, Luke helped me carry the dishes to the kitchen," Elana said. "But we were only back there a second and there wasn't anyone else there."

"I thought you said there was a man?" Kaden said.

"Yeah, but he was at a front table," Elana said.

"What was he wearing?" Kaden asked.

80

24567890

"I don't know," Elana said. "Jeans, a T-shirt. And he had a cowboy hat. Why? What difference does that make?"

"Nothing," Kaden said. Yo-Yo looked at him but Kaden avoided his eyes and hurried into the classroom. Yo-Yo followed after him.

"What's wrong?" Yo-Yo asked. First bell rang. Voices could be heard coming down the hall.

Kaden's eyes met Yo-Yo's. "Dad gave me a used MP3 yesterday."

Second bell rang and class started. Kaden opened his history book but couldn't concentrate. He kept thinking about the MP3 player sitting on his desk at home. Elana's MP3. The one Dad said he got from a friend. By fourth period, he was so upset, he felt sick. He got a pass from Mr. Herd and went to the nurse. The nurse took his temperature, said it was normal, and sent him back to class.

When he got back to Mr. Herd's room, he was surprised Yo-Yo wasn't there. He waited until Mr. Herd turned to write a math problem on the board, then reached across Yo-Yo's empty desk and tapped Elana on the shoulder.

"Where's Yo-Yo?" Kaden whispered.

"Price sent for him," Elana whispered back.

Kaden wasn't alarmed. Mr. Price said he and Yo-Yo were responsible for watering the grass on Tuesdays and Thursdays during lunch. Maybe he had changed his mind.

The bell rang and Kaden headed to the cafeteria. Luke came up behind him in the lunch line.

"Your friend is probably in some deep trouble," Luke said with a smug smile. "Stealing is a felony but you know all about that, don't you?"

Kaden wondered why Luke said *your friend*, not *your dad*, but kept quiet, his eyes on his tray. When he looked up to hand his card to the lunch lady, he saw Yo-Yo sitting in their usual place.

"What did Price want?" Kaden asked.

"I'll tell you when we water," Yo-Yo said. "Grab the hamburger, dump the other stuff, and let's go."

Out in the courtyard, Yo-Yo turned on the hose.

"First of all, you don't have to worry. It wasn't your dad," he said.

"Then who was it?"

"Luke. At least I'm pretty sure but I don't have any proof yet."

"That explains Luke's behavior," Kaden said. "He's been smirking all morning and the only time Luke smirks like that is when he thinks he's gotten away with something. But why did Price want you?"

"Well, Price said he heard a rumor I had an MP3 at

school. Believe me, he is dead set against MP3 players. So he needed to check my backpack and locker."

"You're kidding," Kaden said. "I thought they only did that for drugs."

"Well, evidently, Price includes MP3 players in the category of illegal substances," Yo-Yo said. "Anyway, he searched my backpack and I was thankful I didn't have my MP3 in there today. I usually do but took it out last night to download some more music. But then we went to my locker and Price pulled Elana's MP3 off the top shelf."

"Who put it there?"

"Like I said, I'm pretty sure it was Luke."

"So what did Price say?"

"He told me not to bring it to school again, but since I was a new kid, I was excused this time. He almost said teacher's kid, but caught himself just in time. Principals don't like you to think you can get away with things just because you're a teacher's kid."

"You didn't tell him it was Elana's?"

"No, I didn't want to drag her into it. I'm quite chivalrous, you know."

"Yeah, a regular knight in shining armor." Kaden smiled. "So did you give it to Elana yet?"

"No, Price kept it. He said it's policy to give confiscated

material to parents. He'll give it to my mom after school so I don't have much time to find evidence against Luke."

"So, how do you know Luke took it?"

"Process of elimination. The only people at Pillie's yesterday were Pillie, Elana, Luke, and some stranger. Pillie and Elana are ruled out and the stranger is, too. If the stranger took it, it wouldn't show up in my locker. So that leaves Luke."

"How did Luke get in your locker?"

"That was my stupidity," Yo-Yo admitted. "I was being lazy and didn't want to dial the combination. I just left the lock hanging there. From a distance, it appeared locked but I haven't snapped it shut since the first week of school. Look around when you go down the hall next time. Half the lockers aren't locked."

"How come you didn't tell Price about Luke? He's the one who should get into trouble."

"No proof," Yo-Yo said. "Only my word against his. You have to start watching some of those lawyer shows on TV. You always have to have proof."

That afternoon, as Kaden sat with Kubla in the tower, he thought about the day. He felt bad he had assumed his father was guilty of stealing. For years, he had hated Luke for all his mean comments about his dad.

"But then, when Dad finally gets out of prison, I wasn't any better than Luke," he told Kubla as the bird pulled at his shoelace. "I should apologize but I don't want Dad to know I distrusted him."

Kaden reached out and petted the bird. "Kubla," he continued, "you've always trusted me. Well, from now on, I'm going to try my hardest to be a trusting son."

Dad, Gram, and Kaden sat at the table eating dinner.

"Yesterday I stopped by the diner," Dad said. "Boy, that place has really changed. All those cows and everything."

"I knew you were there," Kaden said. He told Gram and Dad about how Luke tried to make it look like Yo-Yo had stolen Elana's MP3 player. He left out the part about how he suspected Dad of stealing it.

"I saw those two there," Dad said. "They looked like they were having a good time. Why would he want to set Yo-Yo up?"

"Because he's jealous," Kaden said. "Elana and Yo-Yo were having a lot of fun together while planting zoysia grass."

"Why didn't Yo-Yo tell Mr. Price what he suspected about

Luke?" Gram wanted to know.

Dad answered immediately. "Because you don't snitch on your friends."

"I wouldn't exactly call Luke a friend," Gram said.

"Well, you just don't snitch, period," Dad said. "No one likes a snitch."

"The way I see it," Gram said, "no one likes being set up either. And if you didn't do anything wrong, there'd be nothing to snitch on to begin with."

"But you don't tattle," Dad said. "You get even. Isn't that right, Kaden?"

Kaden didn't say anything.

"Cat got your tongue, Kaden?" Gram said. "You must have an opinion one way or the other."

Gram had that patient but expectant look on her face. The look that said "I'm expecting the right answer to come out of your mouth and we can wait here all night until it does." Kaden looked at Dad. He wasn't familiar with his father's looks but the way Dad's eyes were drilling into him, Kaden knew he was waiting for Kaden to side with him.

Kaden looked down at his plate, not wanting to meet his father's eyes. "I don't think Luke should have gotten away with it. It wasn't right. And he'll just think he can get away with more now."

Gram had a satisfied look on her face but Dad balled his hands into fists. He pounded down on the table so hard, all the dishes jumped and a fork clattered to the floor.

"So you're rubbing it in my face, too, huh?" Dad sneered at Kaden, then turned to Gram. "You've been brainwashing this kid against me all along, haven't you?"

"It has nothing to do with you," Gram said. "He was talking about Luke."

Dad didn't say another word. He just shoved back his chair and stomped out the door.

"I didn't mean to upset him," Kaden said to Gram. "I just said what I thought."

"You have nothing to apologize for," Gram said. "Your dad has to realize everything isn't about him. I imagine it hit a nerve with your dad because he knows what he did wasn't right either. Your dad paid for his actions. Luke will, too, sooner or later."

Kaden got up and silently cleared the table. He wished he had never brought the conversation up to begin with. Thinking about what he had said to Kubla that afternoon, he walked over to Cabin Five and knocked on the screen door. Dad didn't answer.

"I wasn't choosing sides," Kaden said through the screen. "I was just saying what I felt."

Dad still said nothing. Kaden stood there several seconds. He didn't want to talk about it anymore but he didn't want his dad to stay mad either.

"You want to play catch before dark?" Kaden changed the subject.

He didn't think his father was going to acknowledge him, and was about to leave when Dad said, "Sure."

Kaden met him on the front lawn, handing over Emmett's glove. After a few throws, Dad finally broke his silence.

"How did your friend get a name like Yo-Yo?" he asked.

It was a legitimate question and Dad didn't say it in a mean way like Luke would have. Dad was obviously trying, too, and as they threw the ball back and forth, Kaden told him all about Yo-Yo.

Wednesday, September 14

CHAPTER TWENTY-EIGHT

PAYING THE PRICE

The next morning, Luke was not on the school bus. Nor was he in Ms. Ales's class first period. Elana wasn't in class either and neither was Yo-Yo. Elana and Yo-Yo both showed up at second period but it wasn't until lunch that Kaden found out what happened.

"Yesterday, after Yo-Yo brought my MP3 to the restaurant and told my mom everything, she called Mr. Price right away," Elana said. "Then we all met this morning: Luke and his dad, me and my parents, Mr. Price and the guidance counselor."

"And Yo-Yo," Kaden added.

"No, I didn't have to be there this morning," Yo-Yo said.

"So where were you?"

"I was singing with first graders." Yo-Yo rolled his eyes. "Boy, that was a lot of fun."

"Why?"

"Price told me to stay in Mom's room first period just in case he needed me and Mom to come in. I told him I didn't mind being in the interrogation without Mom; I could represent myself. They do that a lot on TV but usually it's the bad guy who says he'll be his own lawyer. Price didn't seem too keen on the idea. In fact, he was adamantly against it. He'd make a good judge, you know, like the ones on those real court TV shows. I was just about to ask him if he had ever been a judge, but about that time Mom gave me one of her 'you'd better shut up' looks."

"You need another one now," Kaden said, grinning. "Let Elana talk."

"Well," Elana said, "Luke denied ever touching my MP3, so my parents said they'd ask your dad. They thought he might have seen Luke take it out of my backpack at the restaurant."

"My dad? How did you know that was my dad?"

"I didn't know but Mom did. She remembered he was at the restaurant when Luke and I were there. They knew each other when they were kids," Elana said. "I was surprised you didn't say it was him when I described him."

"You only described his clothes," Kaden said, not wanting

to explain why he hadn't said it was his dad. "Lots of people wear jeans and a cowboy hat. But last night, he told me he had been at the Purple Cow."

"Anyway," Elana continued, "when my dad said they might ask your dad, Luke's dad said . . ." Elana stopped. Her face blushed and she looked away from Kaden uncomfortably.

"It's okay," Kaden said. "I've heard what Luke's dad has said many times."

"Well, what he said wasn't very nice and Mr. Price told him if he didn't stop cussing, he would call in the sheriff and let him handle the whole thing. I guess hearing the word 'sheriff' scared Luke, and he confessed right away."

"So what happened then?" Yo-Yo asked. "Did the sheriff haul him off to jail?"

"No. My parents agreed the sheriff wouldn't be brought into it since Luke's a kid, but he can't come into the Purple Cow anymore."

"So that was it? He steals your MP3 and frames Yo-Yo and then for punishment he can't eat ice cream?" Kaden asked.

"No, there's more," Elana said. "He got in-school suspension and has to stay after school, too. Plus, my parents insisted Yo-Yo get a formal apology from Luke."

"Why in-school suspension?" Yo-Yo asked.

"It started out as regular suspension but Luke made the mistake of opening his mouth, saying he'd like a little vacation. Mr. Woodhead seemed to think that was a pretty good deal, too. So, Price instantly changed his mind. Luke isn't totally kicked out of school but instead of going to regular classes, he has to go to detention."

"Where's that?" Yo-Yo asked.

"Haven't you ever noticed that desk in the corner by Price's door?" Elana asked. "He'll be there all day but has to spend study hall and C.A.R.E. time with the guidance counselor."

"For how long?" Kaden asked.

"Ten days," Elana said. "Price originally said the rest of this week and all of next but Mr. Woodhead said Luke may just be absent all that time, so Price changed it to ten days, not counting any absent days."

Yo-Yo turned to Kaden. "I told you Price would make a good TV judge."

"Well, I've learned one thing," Elana said. "I'm done hanging around with Luke."

The three walked through the library and into the courtyard. Soon all the sixth graders except Luke were planting zoysia grass plugs. After planting a few plugs, Yo-Yo looked toward the far end of the courtyard and gave a little wave.

"Who did you wave to?" Kaden asked.

"Mr. Price," Yo-Yo said. "Until yesterday, I'd never been in his office. Did you know his desk faces out that window?" Yo-Yo pointed to the far end of the courtyard, then waved again. "If he's in there, he can see everything we're doing. It's almost like on the cop shows where they watch suspects through one-way mirrors."

Kaden just shook his head and went back to planting. When all the plugs were planted and the rest of the sixth graders had left, Kaden and Yo-Yo stacked the empty boxes by the door.

"Elana told us about Luke's punishment, but what about you? Did you have to 'pay the price' for not telling that it was Elana's MP3?" Kaden asked.

"I did tell, just not right at first," Yo-Yo said. "Price had already ruined my chance to look for fingerprints when he grabbed the MP3 out of my locker without putting on rubber gloves. So I was trying to gather more evidence but I ran out of time. After school, when I confessed everything to Mom, she marched me right down to Price's office. He didn't have to torture me or anything. Just one look from Price was enough for me to spill my guts."

"You told your mom everything yesterday?" Kaden said.

"Why wouldn't I? I didn't do anything wrong. I was framed. Besides, Mom's a teacher and teachers find out everything. I'd be in big doo-doo if she found out from someone else. Even on TV shows, the cops always tell the captain what they suspect."

"Was your mom mad you didn't tell Price everything right up front?"

"Neither one of them was too happy," Yo-Yo said. "I pleaded my case, stating I was only taking a continuance. That's when you ask the court for more time to gather evidence. I pointed out I would have solved it faster if it hadn't been for Price's evidence tampering. Price wasn't too impressed with my knowledge of the law, though."

"So what was the price?" Kaden asked.

"Price left it up to Mom and Mom-the-parent was influenced by the fact that the crime had to do with MP3 players. So she took mine away for a week for not telling Price it was Elana's. Since the crime occurred at school, Mom-the-teacher suggested I help with the first-grade musical." Yo-Yo moaned. "She thought I was really great with the first graders."

"Well, Gram will be happy," Kaden said. "She wasn't too pleased you didn't tell on Luke."

"I might have made the wrong decision in delaying," Yo-Yo said, "but I wasn't going to just let Luke get away with it. That was never an option."

CHAPTER TWENTY-NINE

STILL STRANGERS

"I'm home!" Kaden yelled when he got off the bus, but walked straight to his cabin. He was dirty again and needed to shower. He went to his dresser to get clean clothes, and sitting on top beside his fan was a cell phone. A note was under it.

Call me. 555-862-1048. —Dad

Kaden put the note down and picked up the phone, wondering whether to tell Gram or not. No matter how he looked at it, someone was going to be angry. Gram at Kaden for keeping secrets. Dad at Kaden for not keeping secrets. Gram at Dad for not getting permission. Dad at Gram for insisting he get permission. Kaden could usually talk with Gram but this time he didn't want to be put in the middle of any more arguments.

Kaden stared at the phone in his hand. He thought about calling Emmett but for the first time in his life he felt he had someone else to turn to. Pocketing the phone, Kaden put the note under his mattress. Then he went to Cabin Four, shut the door, and closed the window.

"Awesome!" Yo-Yo said when he answered the call. "Now we won't have to wait until zoysia watering time to have a private conversation."

"I haven't told Gram yet. Do you think I should? You know how she is about technology. And she's pretty touchy lately about anything involving Dad."

"To tell or not to tell, that is the question," Yo-Yo said dramatically.

"That's what I said," Kaden stated impatiently. "Should I tell her or not?"

"You didn't get it, did you?" Yo-Yo asked.

"I guess not," Kaden replied.

"It's from Shakespeare, or at least kind of. *Hamlet* specifically. My mom took me to see the play last summer. I didn't understand a lot of what they were saying—it was in some old English language—but it was pretty cool. All sorts of murders and some girl drowned and they poisoned people. Everyone died at the end."

"What's that got to do with telling Gram about a cell phone?" Kaden asked.

"Simple," Yo-Yo said. "In the play, Hamlet says, 'To be or not to be, that is the question.' He's trying to figure out whether to live or to kill himself. I told you there's a lot of killing going on in that play. You wouldn't believe it. People are dropping left and right."

"You're making no sense, Yo-Yo," Kaden said.

"Yes, I am. You have to make a decision, just like Hamlet did. Tell her, and you live, but it might be suicide if you don't tell Gram. She'll kill you when she finds out."

"Yeah, I better tell her," Kaden said, laughing. *But not until later*, he thought to himself. *First, I'll call Dad.*

After taking a quick shower, Kaden opened the phone and punched in the number.

"Hey, Kaden," Dad's voice came over the phone, "how do you like your present?"

"It's awesome! Where are you?"

"I'm at the tower. Walk on over, I'll wait for you."

When Kaden got to the muddy spot, he wasn't surprised the leaves were crushed. He knew Dad had driven over them.

When he reached the log barricade, Kubla was on his favorite tree limb, giving warning caws over and over. That didn't surprise Kaden either. Dad was there, and to Kubla, Dad was still a stranger. But there was something that did surprise Kaden. As he walked past Dad's parked truck, he noticed the cargo carrier now had locks on the latches. There'd been no locks when they'd put the TV in it. And when Kaden stepped over the log and headed up the path, he had another surprise. An extension ladder angled from the ground to the first landing.

Kaden looked up. Dad was looking down at him from the top.

As Kaden continued toward the tower, Kubla flew down from the tree, cawing all the way until he landed on Kaden's shoulder. The bird was very agitated. Kaden tried to pet his head to calm him but Kubla wouldn't let him. He jumped over Kaden's head to his other shoulder. He was still making warning noises although they were quieter now. Kaden talked softly to the bird. However, when he started up the ladder, Kubla darted from his shoulder, frantically giving more warning caws. The bird returned to his limb as Kaden went higher and higher but didn't stop the clamorous racket.

"That bird's a pest," Dad said when Kaden climbed through the trapdoor.

"That's Kubla," Kaden said. "He's just trying to warn me that something's wrong. You're a stranger to him."

"I don't know why he still thinks I'm a stranger," Dad said. "I've met him before. And I've been wondering. Why didn't you answer when I called up at you last Saturday?"

Kaden looked at Dad. "I wasn't ready to meet you yet."

"Fair enough but I see you were spying on me. That's a pretty cool periscope in there and I wondered where my binoculars were."

Kaden glanced at the metal chest. An open lock hung from its latch, too.

"Why the lock?" Kaden asked.

"Don't want your stash to disappear, do you? You're not the only one who can get up here, you know."

"What's the combination?" Kaden said.

Dad pulled a slip of paper out of his pocket and handed it to Kaden. "It's on there," he said. Kaden looked at it and put it in his pocket.

"Where'd you get the ladder?" Kaden asked.

"It's Emmett's," Dad answered.

"Really? Emmett loaned you his ladder?" Kaden knew Emmett was very particular about his tools and seldom loaned them out. *If something needs fixing*, Emmett would say, *I'll be happy to help fix it but I won't loan my tools.*

Borrowed tools never seem to find their way back home. Kaden was certain Emmett would include a ladder with things he didn't lend out.

Dad laughed. "I figured the old man was still pretty guardy with his tools. So, let's just say I'm borrowing it."

"Without asking?" Kaden said.

"He won't even miss it. I bet he hasn't moved it in years."

"You should have asked," Kaden said.

"Did you ask me if you could use my binoculars?"

"No," Kaden admitted, "but Emmett asked Gram if he could get them out of your cabin for me."

"Oh, so Emmett took them, huh?" Dad said. "Guess that makes us even."

Kaden didn't like the way the conversation was going. He seemed to have a knack for making Dad angry but Dad was making him angry, as well.

"Take them back, then," Kaden said. "They're yours. I guess I was just borrowing, too."

"No need to get huffy," Dad said. "You can keep them."

Kaden turned to look out the window. Dad sat down. Neither said another word. There was only the constant high-pitched hum of the cicadas. When Dad finally spoke again, his voice had lost that hard edge. "What's all that other stuff in there?"

"Just some things I've found and some stuff I might use up here," Kaden said, sitting down on the opposite side of the tower from his dad. He was glad Dad's mood had suddenly shifted and things seemed to be okay between them again.

"So what do you need baby wipes for?" Dad said. Kaden stretched his legs out and told Dad about the poison ivy and bird poop.

Dad laughed all through the story. When Kaden finished, Dad said, "So are you going to introduce me to that pesky bird of yours?"

Kubla had quieted but was still sitting on his limb. He had not flown over to be with Kaden like he usually did. Kaden got up, took the lock from the latch, and opened the lid of the chest. He rummaged around and came out with a handful of sunflower seeds.

Dad started to stand up but Kaden stopped him.

"He probably won't come if he sees you. Just stay down but hold these." Kaden handed him all but two sunflower seeds.

Without saying a word, Kaden extended his arm out a window, holding up a sunflower seed with his thumb and index finger. Kubla opened his wings and jumped from his limb. With wings flapping like black triangles, Kubla crossed the open space, snatched the sunflower seed, and flew back to his limb.

"Once he eats that," Kaden told Dad, "he'll be back for more but he won't fly away with the next one. Then you can feed him." Kaden sat down on the floor next to Dad.

As Kaden predicted, the crow soon came racing back. He landed on the edge of the window, but seeing Dad, he didn't jump down to Kaden. Kaden put the other sunflower seed in plain view on his outstretched leg. Kubla squawked and jumped sideways along the edge of the window, back and forth, back and forth. He wanted the seed but he was unsure about the stranger.

"I know you don't know him but he's okay," Kaden said softly to Kubla. "He won't hurt you." Kaden nudged the sunflower seed about an inch. "If you want this, you're going to have to come in here to get it."

Kubla couldn't resist. He finally jumped from the window and landed on Kaden's lap. As Kubla grabbed the seed, Kaden put his hands around the bird's wings and petted his head with his thumb, all the time talking calmly.

"Put one of the seeds on your leg," Kaden instructed. Kubla watched Dad but jumped up on Kaden's shoulder when Kaden let him go. The bird muttered in Kaden's ear, jumped on his lap and back to his head, all the while staring at the sunflower seed on Dad's leg.

Finally, Kubla gave in and jumped down on Dad's leg.

Dad reached out to grab the bird like Kaden had done but Kubla gave his hand a hard peck.

"Ouch!" Dad yelled, "you son of a . . ." He instinctively jerked his hand back but then brought it forward again to slap at the bird. Kubla was quicker, though. He took a flying leap to the chest lid and Dad's hand missed. Dad cussed more.

"It wasn't Kubla's fault," Kaden said, getting up and going toward the bird. Kubla jumped onto Kaden's head, muttering and squawking in a perturbed manner. "You scared him trying to grab hold of him like that. And your tone of voice doesn't help much either."

Dad angrily flung the rest of the sunflower seeds across the room. "I wasn't doing anything you didn't do."

"I know, but you're still a stranger to him. It takes time and patience to get to know somebody, you know."

Kaden put out his hand, holding two fingers out together. Kubla jumped from his head and onto Kaden's fingers. Kaden stroked the black feathers with his other hand, quietly cooing and gurgling to him until Kubla cooed and gurgled back. Walking over to where Dad threw the seeds, Kaden squatted down and put his hand close to the seeds. Kubla partially opened his wings to keep his balance, leaned over, and picked up a seed in his beak. Then he sprang from Kaden's fingers and flew from the tower to his limb.

"We better go," Kaden said calmly. "Gram won't like it if we're late for dinner and I still have homework." Kaden put the lock on the latch, twisted the dial, and started down the stairs. Dad followed.

Once down the ladder, Dad headed straight for the truck. Kaden pulled the cord on the ladder to release the extension catches, and the top of the ladder slid down to nestle in with the bottom.

"Just leave that in the weeds over there," Dad called over his shoulder, but Kaden ignored him. He picked the ladder up and carried it to the truck.

"No, you need to take it back to Emmett."

CHAPTER THIRTY

UNDER A YELLOW MOON

Dad didn't say much during dinner but Kaden kept up a steady stream of conversation, telling about his day. He told the details about Luke's, Elana's, and Yo-Yo's visits with Mr. Price. Gram laughed, saying she could see why the first graders loved Yo-Yo. She nodded, indicating she understood when Kaden said Kubla had met Dad but was still uncertain about him. Kaden decided not to mention he knew Kubla would never trust Dad again. He didn't bring up that Dad had taken Emmett's ladder and that it was still in the back of his truck either. Dad now parked his truck in the gap between Cabins Four and Five, and it wasn't visible from Gram's cabin. Kaden wanted to give Dad the chance to take the ladder back without Gram's interference.

They were almost done eating. Kaden had told just about everything that had happened during the day but he knew there was one more thing to tell. The thing that had weighed heavy on his mind all through dinner.

"Have you ever heard of *Hamlet*?" he asked.

"Of course," Gram said. "'To be or not to be, that is the question.' One of Shakespeare's most famous quotes. Why? Are you reading it at school?"

"No, just something Yo-Yo told me. He said he saw the play last summer when I called him this afternoon." Kaden took the phone out of his pocket and put it beside his plate. "Dad gave it to me."

Gram looked at the phone, then at Kaden, then at Dad. "So you were thinking to tell or not to tell, huh?" Gram said.

"Kind of," Kaden admitted, "but I learned a lot from all that stuff with Luke."

"I think your learning is going on the right track," Gram said, nodding. "You can keep the phone but you don't have to go to Cabin Four to talk on it."

Kaden looked up in surprise.

"I was wondering why the window was closed but figured it all out just now when you said you talked to Yo-Yo," Gram said. "Don't close it again. It was all steamy in there. The towels will sour."

Gram turned to Dad. "You've been awful quiet tonight," she said.

"I can give my son a cell phone without your permission if I want," Dad said defensively.

"I never said you couldn't," Gram said.

"And I get the message, you know. All this about Luke and Elana and Kubla and strangers. It doesn't take a rocket scientist to figure out what you're trying to tell me."

"Nobody's trying to tell you anything," Kaden said. "I'm just talking about what went on at school and that's what went on. I tell Gram about my day, every day. Always have."

"There you go again," Dad said. "Just rubbing it in that I haven't been here."

"I'm not trying to rub anything in," Kaden said. "It's just the truth. That's what we've always done. Talked about our day at dinner."

"You haven't been here," Gram said, "and we're not going to pretend you have. Nor are we going to avoid every topic of conversation you might interpret as a personal insult. So face facts and move on. You were in prison. Now you're out. What happens from now on is up to you."

Dad pushed his chair from the table. "I'm going for a drive," he said, standing up.

"Sit back down for a second," Gram demanded. "I have something else I want to say."

Dad didn't leave but he didn't sit back down either. He stood behind his chair, his hand resting on the chair back.

"Getting things for Kaden is fine but there's no need to sneak around about it. Sneaking is for when you're doing something wrong."

"If you're wondering about the phone, I didn't steal it," Dad said. "I bought myself a phone and I put him on my plan. I could put you on so you could have a phone, too, if you want."

"No, thank you," Gram said.

"Have it your way," Dad said. "I was just trying to be nice."

"When I said no, thank you," Gram said. "I meant just that. No, I have no need for a cell phone but thank you anyway."

Kaden noticed how carefully Gram had chosen her words. She wasn't lying. She didn't say she didn't have a cell phone. She said she didn't need one. And she didn't. She already had one. But Kaden wasn't supposed to know that and evidently Dad didn't know Gram had one either. Kaden didn't say a word but wondered why Gram was being sneaky about her phone. All he could think of were Yo-Yo's words, *just in case*, and knew Gram still wasn't sure about how much to trust Dad.

Dad walked out. Gram left the cabin, too. Kaden listened through the kitchen window as he cleared the table. There was no talking. Dad started up the truck and drove away. Gram's glider squeaked as she started muttering to herself.

Kaden finished the dishes and stepped outside. "I've got homework," he told Gram as he crossed the porch.

"It can wait," Gram said. "Sit down here a minute."

Kaden sat down on the glider beside Gram. She put her arm around his shoulders. Slowly they moved back and forth as dusk turned to night.

"Won't be long before it will be too cold to sit out here," Gram said.

"It's only mid-September," Kaden said. "We still have another whole week before fall officially begins."

"A week may seem long to you but when you get older, years seem to fly by pretty fast. It seems like just yesterday your father was your age, sitting here beside me on this glider. I do love him, you know."

They sat for a little longer, the glider moving rhythmically, until Gram spoke again.

"When your grandpa died, it was hard on your dad. He felt lost and lonely and everything made him angry. Including coming up here. He and I came that first summer but we only stayed a week. Emmett tried to help. You know, be a friend, take him fishing and stuff. But your father seemed to resent Emmett was alive and his dad was dead. Your grandfather and Emmett were such very good friends, almost like brothers. And I think your dad was always a little jealous of Emmett. So your dad and I went back to Chapston City and never came back. At least not together. In high school, your dad got in with the wrong crowd and things just got worse. There wasn't anything I did that seemed to make a difference." Gram let out a long sigh.

"How did Grandpa die?" Kaden asked. It was one of the things nobody ever talked about.

"In a car wreck coming back from fishing with Emmett. Your grandfather swerved to avoid a deer, went off the road, and hit a tree. Your grandpa died but Emmett walked away without a scratch."

"Wow," Kaden said. "I knew he and Grandpa were friends but Emmett never told me about that. That must have been awful for him."

"It was," Gram agreed. "For everybody."

"Why hasn't anyone ever told me this?"

"I know there are a lot of things I've kept from you, Kaden. I just needed to wait until I thought you were ready."

They were both quiet for a while as the creaking of the glider mixed with the sounds of evening insects.

"But it's no excuse," Gram finally said.

"What isn't?" Kaden asked.

"That your father's dad died," Gram said. "It's no excuse for doing wrong. Even when things are hard, you still have to be responsible and make the right decisions. For some reason, your dad didn't think the rules applied to him just because he had a hard go of it."

They sat a while longer. A full moon rose, deep yellow, leaving long, crisscrossing shadows of tree branches across the yard and into the circle drive.

"Isn't that pretty?" Kaden said.

"Yes, it is," Gram said. She paused, then spoke again. "I'm proud of you, Kaden. I know it's not easy on you but you're making good choices and you're being patient."

Gram squeezed Kaden's shoulder and gave him a kiss on his forehead. She hadn't done that since first grade when he wasn't invited to Luke's party. "Now go do your homework," she said.

When Kaden went into his cabin, the first thing he did was pull the photo album and notes out from under his mattress. He opened his desk drawer and put them in there. Things in a desk drawer were out of sight but it was a normal place to keep things. Under a mattress was sneaky. Then he sat down at the desk and opened his math book. He was almost done with his homework when he heard Gram open the screen door and go inside.

"Good night, Gram," he said.

"Good night, Kaden."

Kaden heard Gram get a drink of water. Then her voice came over the intercom again. "Only one rule," Gram said. "No calls after nine o'clock."

Kaden looked at his clock. It was 9:35. "Okay," he said.

Thursday, September 15

CHAPTER THIRTY-ONE

THE PLAN

Before eating breakfast, Kaden walked past Cabin Four and looked around the corner. Dad's truck was back but no ladder hung out over the tailgate. When the bus stopped at Emmett's, Doris went inside but Kaden walked behind the shop. The ladder was there, smashing down the weeds.

"Did you see Dad last night?" Kaden asked Emmett when he entered the kitchen.

"No, why?"

"Just curious. Thought he might have come by."

"I doubt your dad's going to come around here much," Emmett said but he didn't say why. Kaden thought he knew the reason but didn't say anything about what Gram told him last night either. Instead, he went over to the wall and looked closely at the pictures. There were a lot of them with Emmett and Grandpa. They were always smiling or laughing.

When it was time to go, Kaden and Doris each grabbed a couple of doughnuts for the road and headed out the door. Emmett followed. "You and Yo-Yo still on for Saturday?"

"Yep," Kaden said.

"Good. Tell Yo-Yo I'll pick him up around nine."

"Sounds like a plan," Kaden said, but on the way to school he came up with a better plan.

"Ask your mom if you can ride home on the bus with me tomorrow and spend the night. Emmett will take you home on Saturday," Kaden told Yo-Yo as soon as he entered Ms. Ales's room.

"Great idea," Yo-Yo said, dumping his backpack. He ran from the room and returned just as second bell rang.

"She said yes," he said, sliding into his seat.

"Super," Kaden said.

"Did you tell Gram?" Yo-Yo asked. Ms. Ales rang the brass bell for silence.

"No," Kaden whispered over Yo-Yo's shoulder, "I'll tell her this afternoon, but I'm sure she won't care. She said you were welcome anytime, remember?"

"Not about spending the night," Yo-Yo said. "About the cell—"

Before Yo-Yo was able to finish his sentence, the announcements blared and all the students rose to say the Pledge of Allegiance. Yo-Yo didn't have a chance to ask about the phone again until lunch.

"So did you tell or not tell, that is the question," Yo-Yo said as they sat down with their trays.

"Told," Kaden said. "I don't relish the idea of suicide. You know Gram; she wouldn't just kill me outright, she'd work me to death."

"So did she get mad? Is she letting you keep it? Will you actually get to talk on it?" Yo-Yo asked without a pause between questions.

"No, yes, and yes," Kaden said, laughing.

Friday, September 16

CHAPTER THIRTY-TWO

HOMEWORK

When Kaden and Yo-Yo got off the bus, Kaden was relieved to see Dad's truck wasn't there, but that was worrisome, also. Yo-Yo wanted to go see Kubla. *What if Dad is at the tower?* Kaden thought. *What if he gets angry again? He's got a pretty short fuse. And Yo-Yo blurts out anything that's going through his head. What if Yo-Yo ticks Dad off?* Kaden was still pondering what to do when Gram put an end to his worries.

"Talking about fall coming the other night got me to thinking," Gram told the boys. "It's time for fall cleaning, and with an extra pair of hands, it will go twice as fast. You can start by straightening up the junk cabin."

"We were going to go to the tower," Kaden complained,

instantly deciding he'd rather chance Yo-Yo seeing Dad get angry than having to do fall cleaning.

"You can go tomorrow morning," Gram said. "Emmett won't want to start working on that wood until morning's half over."

Gram listed what fall cleaning entailed. Neither boy was overjoyed to hear they'd spend the afternoon cleaning seven windows; sweeping five cabin floors plus one porch; and scrubbing five bathroom sinks, five toilets, and one bathtub.

"Sorry," Kaden said as they walked into Cabin One, "but if we work quickly, we may still have a chance to go to the tower before dinner."

"Where's your dad?" Yo-Yo whispered.

"Why are you whispering?" Kaden asked.

"Intercoms," Yo-Yo whispered again, searching the shelves with his eyes.

"There aren't any in here. Just in my room, so stop whispering."

"So where's your dad?" Yo-Yo said again, but louder this time.

"I don't know. He goes to Chapston City a lot to look for work."

"That's boring," Yo-Yo said.

"Shh!" Kaden said, looking toward the open door. "If she

hears that word, we'll have more work to do. Gram hates that word."

"What word?" Yo-Yo asked.

"The B-word," Kaden said.

Yo-Yo thought for a moment. "You mean 'boring'?"

"Shhhhh, I'm serious." But the laughter in Kaden's voice said otherwise. Kaden handed Yo-Yo a broom and the two boys quickly cleaned the first four cabins.

"So, the infamous Cabin Five," Yo-Yo said as they left Cabin Four. "Have you been in it yet?"

"Nope," Kaden said. "Only talked to Dad through the screen door once."

"So we head to uncharted lands," Yo-Yo said, but as they walked past Cabin Five's window, Yo-Yo stopped. "Do you think he'll mind us snooping around in his cabin?"

"We're not snooping; we're cleaning," Kaden said, although he was wondering the same thing.

Both boys became silent as Kaden slowly turned the key Gram had given him and pushed open the door. He took one tentative step forward and stopped.

Inside there was a bed, a desk, and a dresser. The furniture was identical to Kaden's. A fan sat on top of the dresser, its blades spinning. The bed was not made. The top sheet was wadded up at the foot of the bed and a blanket and quilt lay in a heap on the floor. Clothes were scattered around, too.

"I guess Gram can't force a grown man to keep his room clean," Kaden said, and stepped farther in. Yo-Yo followed on tiptoes, not making a peep.

Unlike Kaden's room, there was nothing on the walls. On the desk was a ceramic pot with thick, uneven, and wobbly sides. Its reddish-brown glaze had dripped during firing, leaving a darker, thicker line down one side. Kaden picked it up and looked inside. A few coins, an old, rusty fishing lure, and a couple of rocks with fossils in them. All dust-covered. He could feel something was scratched in the bottom. Putting his hand over the top, he turned it over. There was a date and Dad's initials. Kaden smiled. He had made a pinch pot when he was eight, too. As Kaden turned it back over, one of the rocks fell out and landed with a thud on the wooden floor. Yo-Yo let out a yelp and sprang backward, tripping over a pair of shoes. He landed hard on the bed and the bed caved in.

"What is your problem?" Kaden said.

"You startled me," Yo-Yo said. "I'm a little on edge here."

"Oh, for crying out loud, it was just a rock."

Kaden put the clay pot back on the desk and pulled Yo-Yo up.

"Help me with the mattress," he said. He lifted one side and Yo-Yo picked up the other and they leaned it against the desk, the top sheet sliding down on the floor. Then they picked up the box spring and leaned it against the mattress. One of the wooden slats that went across the bed frame was broken. The other slats had also fallen to the floor. Kaden picked up the broken slat and put the two pieces just outside the door.

"Two slats will probably do until Emmett can fix that," he said. "I'll take it with us tomorrow."

The boys evenly spaced the unbroken slats on the bed frame and put the box spring and mattress back.

Kaden pulled the bottom sheet from the mattress. "We might as well put on clean sheets," he said. "Go get some. They're in Cabin Four. And put these in the wash." Kaden stuffed the sheets and some dirty clothes into Yo-Yo's arms. "Do you know how?"

"I have to do chores at my house, too, you know," Yo-Yo answered as he pushed open the screen door.

Kaden turned back to the desk. The only other things on it were a few cash register receipts. He picked one up. It was for the TV. He thought about what Luke said. The receipt would prove his dad paid for the TV with his credit card but Kaden didn't need to prove anything to Luke. He put it back on the desk.

The desk drawer was open just a crack. Not even enough to stick out beyond the lip of the desktop. Kaden absently pushed it closed but then thought of his own trick with the stick and the muddy spot. Maybe Dad left the drawer just barely open to see if anyone had been in his desk. Kaden opened it again, just a crack. Then, curiosity getting the best of him, he pulled it wide open.

Inside was just the usual desk stuff. Two pens, a pencil, a few broken crayons, a pair of child's scissors, an eraser with a hole roughly dug into the middle of it, its edges rounded from use, and a small bottle of glue, long dried out. Stuffed in the very back corner was an old black leather wallet.

Kaden pulled it out. There was nothing in it except a card that comes with new wallets to put identification information on. Like the wallet, it was worn and creased. The ink was faded but Kaden could still see the writing on it. It said *Michael Smith* and had a Chapston City address.

He must have been one of Dad's old friends, Kaden thought. *Maybe Dad invited him to come with him to the cabins when he was younger.* He put it back and closed the drawer, leaving it open a bit, just as he had found it.

Kaden turned to the dresser. There wasn't much in it either. The top drawer had socks and underwear; the second, T-shirts; the third had a pair of shorts and a pair of jeans. Unlike the things in the desk drawer, all the clothes looked very new. Kaden had just opened the fourth drawer when a deep voice behind him said, "Get out of there!"

Startled, Kaden jumped up and spun around. Yo-Yo stood outside the screen door, laughing.

"Man, did you jump!" Yo-Yo said, stepping inside. "Thought you said we weren't snooping. Find anything interesting?"

"Nope." The fourth drawer was empty and Kaden pushed it closed. "I guess Gram was right. Emmett took out the only thing of any importance."

"Have you searched the closet yet?" Yo-Yo asked.

"No."

Yo-Yo opened the closet door. Hanging inside were three shirts, a jean jacket, and two empty hangers. Wadded up in the corner were a few more T-shirts and several pairs of underwear and socks. Kaden gathered them up and put them by the screen door. When they finished cleaning, Kaden picked up the pile of laundry to take to Cabin Four but Yo-Yo grabbed one of the T-shirts and started rubbing the closet doorknob.

"What are you doing?" Kaden asked.

"Fingerprints," Yo-Yo said, holding up his hand and wiggling his fingers. "I'm erasing evidence."

Gram was waiting on the porch. "You guys did a good job."

"Thanks," Kaden said. "Can we go to the tower for a little while?"

"I've got a better idea," Gram said. "Let's build a campfire, instead. We'll roast hot dogs for dinner."

"That'd be cool," Yo-Yo piped up.

"We need to invite Emmett, too," Kaden added.

"Well, run down there and ask him," Gram said.

"No," Kaden said. "I can give him a call. Remember?"

Gram nodded. "This will be fun. We haven't had a cookout in a long time."

Kaden went to his cabin and took the cell phone from his desk. "Hi, Emmett!"

Emmett was surprised to hear Kaden's voice. "Is everything okay?" he said right away.

"Everything's fine," Kaden said. "Just asking if you want to come roast hot dogs with us?"

"Hot diggety dogs," Emmett whooped. "I'll be right up. So, Gram told you about her phone, did she?"

Kaden put his hand over the intercom before answering.

"No, I'm using mine," he said very quietly. "Dad gave me one yesterday. Gram hasn't said a word about hers."

After Kaden hung up, he and Yo-Yo gathered sticks and branches in the woods. They had quite a pile next to the old stone fireplace when Emmett pulled in.

"So, is it going to be a box or a tepee?" Emmett asked as the boys helped him carry logs from his truck to the fireplace.

"Tepee," Kaden stated.

"What are you talking about?" Yo-Yo asked.

"How we're going to build the fire," Kaden said. "Haven't you ever built a fire before?"

"My dad uses a gas grill. All you do is push a button."

"Well, then, we'll have a little outdoor education," Emmett said. "I haven't gotten to teach someone how to light a fire in years."

Emmett started showing Yo-Yo how to light a fire while Kaden went to help Gram. When he came out, Emmett was telling Yo-Yo about combustion and energy.

"Emmett knows all sorts of stuff about energy," Kaden stated, bringing chairs from the porch. "He was a rocket scientist."

"You're kidding? Really?" Yo-Yo asked.

"An aerospace engineer, actually," Emmett corrected.

"Did you go up into space?" Yo-Yo asked.

"No, I just helped design the rockets used to take people into space."

"Wow!" Yo-Yo said. "I thought you just fished and made signs."

"You can't judge a book by its cover," Emmett said. "People can be interested in more than one thing, and the more you're interested in, the more interesting your life. Right now, I'm interested in getting this fire going, because I know later I'm going to be more interested in some s'mores."

"You brought stuff for s'mores?" Kaden asked excitedly. "All right!"

"Let's get this baby lit," Yo-Yo said. "There's s'more to be interested in than standing around talking."

Yo-Yo grabbed the box of matches but Emmett took them from him.

"Hang on there, space cadet." Emmett pulled out one matchstick and formally held it up. "The true test of the fire builder is whether he can light it with just one match." Emmett instructed Yo-Yo, and soon flames were leaping from the fireplace.

"You are now an official fire builder," Emmett stated as Gram came out with a tray full of food. Yo-Yo helped Kaden carry over the glider and the evening was spent roasting hot dogs and marshmallows, telling stories, and singing songs.

CHAPTER THIRTY-THREE

A LITTLE STIRRING UP

Dusk had turned to dark and the fire had died down. The logs glowed with embers that pulsed as if alive. Everyone had quieted, just watching the fire, which occasionally flared up and then died down again. Kaden pointed out a log that looked like an alligator, its eye flickering red. Yo-Yo found a dragon sporadically breathing flames.

Suddenly Gram jumped up and went around to the other side of the fireplace and picked up a long stick.

"Uh-oh," Emmett said. "She's getting a poker stick. She'll be putting the fire out for sure now."

"I'm not going to put out the fire. It just needs a little stirring up."

"You're the perfect one to do that," Emmett joked. "You're always stirring something up."

Gram poked and pushed at the glowing logs. All the embers turned black.

"See what I said," Emmett stated. "She's put it out."

Using the stick like a lever, Gram moved the logs around some more. Sparks danced up into the air and the logs burst into flames.

"Never hurts to stir things up a bit," she stated, putting the poker stick down.

"Well, looks like things are going to get stirred up a little bit more and pretty quickly, too." Emmett nodded toward the road. The roadway was black but the telephone wires and treetops were lit up. Within seconds, headlights came up over the hilltop and the white pickup slowed down to turn into the circle drive.

"I think I'll call it a night. You boys make sure you douse this fire and stir the ashes before going to bed. Thanks for the evening, Greta. See you boys in the morning." Emmett got up and picked up the tray with the leftover food on it. "I'll take this in for you on my way."

Dad pulled his pickup between Cabins Four and Five. As he walked over toward the fire, Emmett came out of Gram's cabin and they passed each other.

"Dennis," Emmett said, tipping his hat.

Dad walked past without speaking. He came over to the fire and sat down on the glider next to Gram.

"You could have spoken," Gram said after Emmett pulled out.

Dad ignored her. "Great night for a fire," he said pleasantly. "Got anything to eat out here?"

"There's a couple of hot dogs left but they're in the house," Kaden answered.

It wasn't until Dad stood up that he noticed Yo-Yo.

"So who do we have here?" he asked.

"That's my friend, Yo-Yo," Kaden said. "I've told you about him. Yo-Yo, this is my dad."

Kaden hoped his dad wouldn't say anything about Yo-Yo's name. He was relieved when Dad just put out his hand and said he was glad to meet him.

"Glad to meet you, too, Mr. McCrory," Yo-Yo said as he stood up and shook Dad's hand. "I've heard a lot about you. I mean, not a lot, not like a biography or anything, but some, you know, like about as much as on the back of a book jacket, where it tells who the author is and where he lives and that you have a son and when you're not writing you like to play golf or something, not that you are a writer or play golf but that's the kind of stuff on the back of a book jacket and that's how much I've heard about you, some but not a whole lot. . . ."

Dad just stared at Yo-Yo, who was still holding his hand, pumping it rapidly up and down, but Gram and Kaden both started laughing.

"Okay, Yo-Yo, you can sit down now," Gram said, interrupting him.

Yo-Yo stopped talking and sat back down. He sat so straight and his muscles were so tense that Kaden felt all it would take would be for someone to poke him lightly with a stick and he would fly out of his seat like a rocket. When Dad left to get some hot dogs, Yo-Yo slumped back in his chair and let out his breath.

"I was just a little on edge," he said to Gram. "Do you think he noticed?"

"No," Gram said. Kaden could tell from her voice she was trying not to laugh again. "Probably just a little too much sugar from all those s'mores."

Gram got up from the glider. "I'm going to turn in, too. Remember what Emmett said about the fire."

When Dad returned, the flames had died to embers again. He loaded the hot dog fork and stuck it out over the glowing coals.

"Stir that up a little, Kaden," he said. "I like my hot dogs blackened."

"I don't," Yo-Yo said. Dad and Kaden both looked at Yo-Yo, wondering if he was going to burst into another frantic speaking bout, but he didn't. "I like them slow roasted, just pinkish brown."

"What about you, Kaden?" Dad asked.

"Yo-Yo and I are opposites. I like hot dogs burned, like you, but I want my marshmallows toasted golden brown. Yo-Yo likes to catch marshmallows on fire."

"Gram said a little charcoal is good for thy stomach's sake," Yo-Yo said.

"But Gram eats hers golden brown," Kaden said to Yo-Yo. "She didn't accept any of the ones you offered to her."

"But Emmett ate his burned," Yo-Yo said. "What about you, Mr. McCrory, do you like golden or burned marshmallows?"

At the mention of Emmett's name, Kaden cringed but Dad didn't get upset this time.

"Call me Dennis," he said. "I like mine burned if I'm just popping them in my mouth, golden if they're for s'mores. Speaking of which, do you guys want some more s'mores?"

Kaden and Yo-Yo both cracked up.

"What's so funny?" Dad asked.

"All evening long, Yo-Yo has been asking over and over if anyone wanted some more s'mores. It became so annoying Gram told him she was going to buy s'more zoysia grass if he said s'more some more."

"I just think it sounds cool and wanted to say s'more some more," Yo-Yo said.

"Gram," Kaden yelled, "you need to get s'more zoysia grass!"

"They tricked me into it!" Yo-Yo yelled. "I didn't mean to say s'more some more."

Gram stuck her head out her screen door. "I don't want to hear any s'more yelling," she said, smiling. "You'll wake the neighbors."

Kaden chuckled but Yo-Yo laughed so hard, he fell out of his chair. Then he suddenly jumped up, said, "I've got to pee," and raced to Kaden's cabin.

"That's some friend you have there," Dad said. "A little high-strung."

"Yeah, but we have a good time," Kaden said. They were quiet for a few seconds and then Dad spoke up.

"I've been thinking about Wednesday night and I want to apologize. I know you weren't trying to rub anything in. I'm just a little touchy and need to lighten up some. I'm going to try harder from now on. I hope you believe me."

"That's okay, Dad. It's going to take us all a little time to get used to one another."

"You know, that's the first time you've called me Dad. It sounded good."

Kaden looked at his father. "It felt good, too."

"So, besides having a campfire, what have you two been up to today?" Dad asked as Yo-Yo came walking back.

"Nothing much," Kaden answered. "Just school and then fall cleaning."

"Fall cleaning?" Dad asked.

"Yeah, Gram had us clean all the cabins after school."

"That's no fun," Dad said.

"It wasn't that bad," Yo-Yo said. "They're not very big, so there wasn't much to clean. Yours was the worst." He had started talking at a normal pace but now he sped up a mile a minute. "I mean it wasn't really dirty or anything, it was just messy, you know, with clothes scattered all over and then we had to change the sheets when the bed broke. Oops!"

Yo-Yo clamped his hand over his mouth.

"Oops?" Dad asked.

"It's okay, Yo-Yo." Kaden laughed, then turned to Dad. "Yo-Yo tripped and landed on your bed and the whole thing went crashing in. We put it back together, but be careful getting in. It only has two slats now. One broke but Emmett can fix it."

Dad had been laughing about Yo-Yo falling on the bed but his laughter suddenly ceased.

"I don't need Emmett to fix it; I can fix it myself."

There was silence. Kaden got up and tossed in a small log.

"I think we need s'more wood on the fire," Kaden said, trying to lighten up the situation.

"And I think it needs s'more poking," Yo-Yo said. He jumped up so fast to grab the poking stick that his chair tumbled over backward.

"I know what you two need s'more of. You need s'more fun," Dad said. His voice was friendly once again. "Fall cleaning isn't what two boys should be doing on a Friday afternoon. How would you guys like to go to Amazon Amazement tomorrow?"

"Sweet!" Kaden exclaimed. "That'd be super!"

"What's Amazon Amazement?" Yo-Yo asked.

"It's an amusement park," Kaden answered.

"I love amusement parks," Yo-Yo said. "What's this one like?"

"I've never been there," Kaden said, "but I've heard kids talk a lot about it at school. Everything is like you're in the Amazon rainforest. They've got rides with piranhas that snap out of the water at you and a roller coaster that goes all around through a jungle and even a ride where they strap you in and you glide on a cable from tree to tree like Tarzan."

"Wicked," Yo-Yo said. "Count me in but I have to be home by six."

"Not a problem," Dad said. "We'll just leave early to get in a full day. They open at eight and it takes about an hour and a half to get there. So, let's leave at six fifteen. We can grab some breakfast at a drive-through. I'm sure you boys would like something besides oatmeal."

"Sounds great to me," Kaden said.

"Well, we'd better get to bed, then," Dad said. Kaden took the poker and started spreading the glowing logs around the fireplace.

"You don't need to do that," Dad said. "It will just burn out."

"Emmett told us to douse the fire before we went to bed," Kaden said without thinking.

"Emmett doesn't know everything," Dad said, sounding irritated again. "Just leave it."

"No, Yo-Yo's never had a fire. He needs to learn how to douse it," Kaden said, hoping to draw Dad away from the subject of Emmett. He turned to Yo-Yo. "When you first dump water on it, it looks just like a volcano steaming up."

Kaden ran over to the side of Gram's cabin, turned the spigot, and dragged the hose across the drive to the fireplace. He sprayed water on the fire and steam gushed from the hot coals but gradually it steamed no more. Kaden kept pouring on more water as Yo-Yo stirred the black ashy soup with the poking stick. Suddenly Kaden thought of something else.

"I just remembered! We can't go tomorrow," he said to Dad. "We told Emmett we'd help him split wood."

"For crying out loud," Dad said. "You boys shouldn't be spending Saturday splitting wood."

"It's a lot of work for Emmett to do it by himself anymore," Kaden explained, "so we said we'd help."

"If Emmett's too old to do it himself, he should just give it up. Call him and tell him you can't come."

"I guess I could," Kaden said. "He probably won't mind if I help him on Sunday instead."

"You don't have to help him at all," Dad said. "He's just using you for free labor while cashing in for himself."

Dad was steaming up and Yo-Yo was stirring the ashes like he was trying to stir a hole to China.

"No, he pays me. And he gives a lot of the wood away for free. Besides, I don't mind helping. Gives me a good workout." Kaden flexed his arms to show his biceps, hoping that would keep Dad from reigniting. He didn't say that pay was just a visit to Pillie's. That would be certain to stir Dad into another big flare-up.

"That old man doesn't have any say in who you choose to spend your weekend with. He's just interfering in my life again. I'm your father and I told you to call him."

"Yes, sir," Kaden said respectfully as Dad walked off toward Cabin Five.

"Whoa," Yo-Yo said quietly once Dad's screen door closed. "I thought I was going to witness Mount Vesuvius erupting."

"Yeah, he does have a temper but it's usually just when Emmett is brought up."

"What's with it between those two?" Yo-Yo asked.

"I don't know," Kaden said. He understood about Dad resenting Emmett surviving the car wreck but that was a long time ago. It didn't make sense Dad would still be so angry. Kaden couldn't figure out why Emmett was so cold to Dad either. "But it's definitely something and it would probably be best to avoid saying Emmett's name tomorrow. And by the way, let's keep another volcano from erupting. Gram isn't too thrilled with amusement parks. She thinks there's plenty around here to amuse ourselves with. So that would be a word to avoid, too."

"Amusement parks and boring," Yo-Yo said, and started humming the theme song to *Jeopardy!* "What are two things we won't say in front of Gram?"

"There's a bunch of things you shouldn't say in front of Gram." Kaden laughed.

"I bet she has a whole alphabetical list," Yo-Yo said.

As the boys pulled the hose back across the driveway and looped it around the holder on the side of Gram's cabin, they continued naming things Gram didn't like in alphabetical order. Computers, dryers, electric can openers, field trips, gibberish . . . The list went on and on until they reached the letter "Z." Neither could think of something Gram didn't like that started with "Z."

"But we know what she does like," Yo-Yo said, "zoysia grass."

Back in his cabin, Kaden picked up his cell phone, then looked at the clock. Ten fifty-two. Gram had said no calls after nine but if he turned off the intercom, she'd never know. Kaden reached over and pushed the button. The light turned black. He stood there, phone in hand, but then put the phone back on his desk.

"It's too late to call Emmett," he told Yo-Yo. "He'll be in bed already. I'll call him in the morning."

"My mom will still be up, though," Yo-Yo said, pulling his cell phone from his duffel bag.

While Kaden brushed his teeth, Yo-Yo called his mom and told her where he would be going. He also talked her into an extra hour at the amusement park. After he hung up, Yo-Yo set the alarm on his phone, put it on Kaden's desk, and both boys went to bed.

Kaden was almost asleep when he remembered. Jumping out of bed, he went to his desk. When he climbed back in bed, the red light on the intercom was glowing again.

Saturday, September 17

CHAPTER THIRTY-FOUR

NOT AMUSED

The alarm on Yo-Yo's cell phone went off at exactly six o'clock, a bugle loudly playing reveille. Gram's voice instantly came over the intercom.

"What in tarnation is that?"

Yo-Yo sprang to the desk and turned off the alarm. "It's the alarm on my cell phone," he explained. "I like to pretend I'm in the army."

"Well, get dressed and march on over here. I'll get the oatmeal cooking," Gram said.

"We're not eating oatmeal this morning," Kaden called from bed. "We're going to spend the day with Dad. He said we'll get some breakfast at a drive-through."

"I bet that's on the list," Yo-Yo whispered.

"What list?" Gram asked. Yo-Yo mouthed "oops" and popped both hands over his mouth.

"Nothing," Kaden said. "You know how Yo-Yo is full of gibberish." Yo-Yo threw a pillow at Kaden. Kaden threw it back but Yo-Yo ducked and the pillow landed on the desk, on top of both cell phones and the intercoms.

"Where is your dad taking you?" Gram asked, but her voice was muffled under the pillow and the boys didn't hear.

"Hey, I brought this, too," Yo-Yo said, pulling a bunch of cords and earbuds from his duffel bag. "We can listen in the truck."

"I thought your mom took your MP3 away from you," Kaden said.

"She did but she didn't say anything about my adapter or earbuds," Yo-Yo said. "Or about listening to *your* MP3."

Kaden grabbed his MP3 player and dumped it in Yo-Yo's duffel bag. He went back to his dresser and pulled a pair of sunglasses from the top drawer just as Dad opened the screen door.

"You guys ready?" he asked.

"Ready, Freddy," Yo-Yo said.

They darted out the door.

"Bye, Gram!" Kaden yelled as he and Yo-Yo raced past

her cabin.

"Thanks for letting me spend the night!" Yo-Yo yelled, too.

As Dad walked past her cabin, he too called out. "I'm taking Yo-Yo home at six. We'll be back for supper."

The three piled into the truck and they pulled out of the driveway.

"I don't have to be home by six anymore," Yo-Yo said. "I talked Mom into seven."

"Good," Dad said. "We can stay at the park until closing."

Yo-Yo rummaged through his duffel bag and pulled out the MP3 player and adapter. He handed the adapter to Kaden. Kaden plugged it into the truck and looked up just as Emmett's welcome signs came into view.

"Oh no," Kaden said. "I forgot to call Emmett this morning. It was too late last night. Can you pull in real quick so I can let him know?"

Dad kept on driving. "Just give him a call," he said.

"I didn't bring the phone," Kaden said.

"Why not? Why do you think I got one for you?" Dad said. "There's no point of having one if you don't bring it."

"I didn't think of it. I'm not used to having one."

"You can use mine," Yo-Yo said. He searched through his duffel bag but came up empty-handed. "Darn, I left it on your desk. Remember, I had it out for the alarm clock."

"Can I use yours, Dad?" Kaden asked.

"I forgot mine, too," Dad said. Kaden noticed the smirk on Dad's face.

He wanted everything to go smoothly. They were almost to town now and asking Dad to turn back would only aggravate him, especially since it pertained to Emmett.

"That's okay," Kaden said. "Emmett was going to come pick us up around nine. Gram will tell him." Kaden was going to add Emmett would understand but decided not to light another fire.

Dad pulled into the parking lot at Amazon Amazement. Before getting out, he pulled out his wallet and handed it to Yo-Yo.

"Put this in the glove box," he said. "I don't want to lose it on any of the rides."

Yo-Yo opened the glove box and put it in. Kaden noticed there were two other wallets in the glove box as well.

"You better put your MP3 out of sight, too," Dad said. "You don't want someone to break in and steal it."

Surprised, both Kaden and Yo-Yo stared at Dad. "Well, that's how it's done, you know."

Kaden knew Dad had been in prison for stealing but he never really thought about him actually doing it. He didn't have time to think about it for long, because Yo-Yo started up.

"I'll put it in here," he said, cramming it and all its cords into the glove box. "But what should I do with my duffel bag? Should I leave it in plain sight? It won't fit under the seat but doesn't have anything important in it, just a smelly T-shirt and some clean underwear my mom insisted I bring. She always says I should have two extra pairs just in case. I think that comes from when I was a baby and really needed some just in case, but I'm still wearing the same ones I had on yesterday and nobody would want to steal underwear anyway, but you can't see if there's anything else in here someone would want to . . ."

Dad looked at Yo-Yo and said, "Zip it."

Yo-Yo stopped talking and held the duffel bag upside down. Nothing fell out. "It is zipped."

"He means your mouth," Kaden said.

Before Yo-Yo could say another word, Dad reached over and grabbed the duffel bag.

"I'll put it in back. You guys go on up to the ticket window. I'll meet you there."

Dad got out of the truck. Yo-Yo shut the glove box and the two boys got out. They had started toward the ticket booth when Kaden thought about the sunglasses he was wearing.

"I'll be right back," Kaden said to Yo-Yo. "I don't want to lose these on the rides either."

Kaden jogged back to the truck. Dad had unlocked the cargo carrier and was lifting the lid.

"Here. Put these in there, too," Kaden said, jumping up on the back bumper and leaning over the tailgate to hand Dad his glasses. Dad quickly dropped the lid but it was too late. Kaden already had a good look inside.

There was a bunch of stuff in the carrier now. A drill, a circular saw, a few other power tools, and one thing Kaden recognized: one of Emmett's toolboxes. Kaden knew it was his. It was dark green with a Trout Unlimited sticker on it.

"What's all that stuff in there?" Kaden asked.

"I'm doing some construction work," Dad said to Kaden. He locked the carrier and walked off.

Kaden didn't move but as his father walked away, he called out, "Why do you have Emmett's toolbox?"

Dad stopped and turned around. Another big smirk crossed his face. He glared directly in Kaden's eyes and said, "I'm borrowing it."

Dad walked rapidly away and caught up with Yo-Yo, who stood near the ticket booth, unfolding a map of the park.

"Come on," Yo-Yo called out impatiently to Kaden. "They're opening the gates."

Kaden walked slowly toward them.

"Two children, one adult," Dad said as Kaden walked up. He handed the girl a credit card.

"We should go here first," Yo-Yo told Kaden. He pointed out a ride on the map but Kaden was thinking about the toolbox.

"I'll need some identification," the girl said.

Dad's hand went to his back pocket. "Oh, heck, I left my wallet in the truck," he told the girl pleasantly, a big smile across his face. "Didn't want it to fall out on the rides. Do I have to have it? I can send one of the boys back for it."

"No, that's okay," the girl said. "A lot of people leave them in their cars." She processed the credit card, handed him a slip to sign, and gave him a receipt. "Show that to the man at the gate and he'll stamp your hands."

"Thank you," Dad said.

Kaden hadn't been paying much attention to what Dad was saying to the girl but he distinctly heard her last words to his father. It felt like someone had knocked the wind out of him.

"Thank you, Mr. Adams."

Pocketing the credit card, Dad turned to the boys.

"Can we do the Amazon River Ride first?" Yo-Yo asked. It was obvious to Kaden that Yo-Yo hadn't heard the girl's words. "It's the one with the piranhas. Can we do it first? Can we? Can we?" Yo-Yo was jumping up and down, he was so excited.

Kaden wanted to join in and be as excited as Yo-Yo but he couldn't. He couldn't get the girl's words out of his head. Without even having to see it, Kaden knew the credit card had *Emmett Adams* stamped on the bottom. He also knew the green toolbox shouldn't be in the cargo carrier. He looked at his dad reading over the map. Dad didn't seem to be a bit bothered about what he had done.

Kaden could feel anger rising up inside of him. He wanted to confront his father but just like he had done at the tower when his dad first called out his name, he froze. With smiling people streaming past him, Kaden stood there, his fists clinched tight, wondering what he should do.

Yo-Yo grabbed Kaden by the arm. "Come on," he said, dragging Kaden toward the Amazon River Ride.

Before they reached the ride, Kaden decided he would say boat rides made him seasick and insist Dad and Yo-Yo go without him. Then he would have some time to figure out what to do. But Dad beat him to the draw, dashing his plans.

"You boys go on, I'm going to wait this one out. I really don't want to get wet."

Kaden got in line with Yo-Yo.

"What's the matter?" Yo-Yo asked.

"Nothing," Kaden replied, trying to force a smile. "This will be a blast."

As they rode through thick tropical foliage, 3-D images of piranhas came out from nowhere, with snapping jaws appearing to be inches away from biting off their arms, legs, and heads. Deep in his own thoughts, Kaden hardly noticed them but Yo-Yo screamed and startled at every lunge, making the raft pitch to and fro and water pour over his head.

"You look like a drowned rat," Dad teased Yo-Yo when they got off the ride. "Your mom may be right. You may need those extra pairs of underwear after all."

"I'm glad we don't have a camera. I don't need another embarrassing picture to add to Emmett's wall," Yo-Yo said. Kaden shot a worried look at his father but this time Dad didn't seem irritated at the mention of Emmett. In fact, he acknowledged him.

"I remember Emmett's wall," Dad said. "And that's a good idea. There's a gift shop over there. Let's go buy a camera."

Yo-Yo moaned but had a huge smile on his face as they followed Dad across to the gift shop. Dad didn't pick out a cheap throwaway camera. He chose a digital camera. The most expensive one in the display case. Kaden stayed close to Dad's side as the woman rang it up. He wanted to take a good look at the credit card to see if it really said *Emmett Adams* on it. *Maybe I just heard wrong*, Kaden hoped. *Or maybe the girl thought Dad looked like someone else. Some other Mr. Adams.* Kaden looked carefully at the card Dad handed the woman. It didn't say *Emmett Adams*. This time the card said *Michael Smith*.

On the next ride, only two people could ride together. Kaden convinced Dad to go with Yo-Yo. As they left, Dad handed Kaden the camera.

Kaden sat down on a bench. *I should take it back*, he thought. But as soon as he got in the gift shop, he had second thoughts. *Dad will want to know where it is.*

He stood in the middle of the shop, his stomach feeling like it was being twisted into a knot.

"Is something wrong?" the woman behind the counter asked. "Do you want me to call security?"

Kaden never thought of contacting security but thinking about it now made him more anxious and more indecisive.

"No, nothing's wrong," he said quickly, and ran back out. Yo-Yo and Dad were just getting off the ride, both laughing.

"You've got to go on that with me, Kaden," Yo-Yo said, pulling him to the line. "It was so amazing but I'm not going to tell you a thing. You've got to experience it."

Normally Kaden would have loved the ride but all the surprise twists and turns and dips and dives left his already churned-up stomach feeling even worse. When they got off, Yo-Yo went running up to Dad, who was waiting on a bench.

"Kaden threw up," Yo-Yo said, "but thank goodness not on the ride. In the trash can over there at the exit gate."

Yo-Yo pointed to Kaden, who was wiping his mouth with a tissue some woman had given him. Dad stayed on the bench.

"He'll be okay," Dad said. "I didn't know he was such a wimp. But there's a movie about rainforests. We'll go watch that to give his stomach a chance to calm down for a while."

They had to buy extra tickets to see the movie. Kaden and Yo-Yo stood to the side while Dad went up to the ticket window. Yo-Yo chatted on and on but Kaden didn't listen. He just watched intently as his father reached into his pocket and pulled out a credit card. It was Emmett's again. Kaden knew by the color. Emmett's card was brown. Michael Smith's was blue. Kaden's stomach tightened again.

In the theater, Kaden stared unseeingly at the screen. Like Yo-Yo with Luke, he knew he wouldn't let Dad get away with it. That wasn't an option. He also knew he didn't want to do it here, in front of Yo-Yo and all these people. Walking out of the theater, he had a plan and that made him feel somewhat better.

For the rest of the day, Kaden did his best to avoid having any confrontations with Dad. Going on rides with Yo-Yo made that easy to do but just about every time they got off

a ride, Dad stood waiting with something in his hands—
hamburgers, sodas, ice-cream bars—and Kaden felt the
sinking pit in his stomach growing deeper and deeper.

"Don't sit this one out, Dad," Kaden pleaded at each ride.
Dad looked pleased Kaden was begging him to join them. To
anyone listening, it would have sounded like the boy really
liked being with his father. But Kaden felt sick whenever Dad
turned him down. He wasn't disappointed his father wouldn't
go on rides with him; he just wanted to keep Dad from using
the credit cards. But when Kaden and Yo-Yo got off the last
ride of the day, Dad was waiting with two intricately carved
lizards, one for each of them.

"Sweet!" Yo-Yo said excitedly. "Thanks!"

"Yeah," Kaden said emptily. He had no room left for
pretend enthusiasm.

"You don't sound too thrilled," Dad said. "Would you
rather have something else?"

"No, I just don't feel good, that's all," Kaden said truth-
fully. "It's been a long day."

On the way home, Yo-Yo fell right to sleep. Kaden thought
that seemed like a good idea. By sleeping, he could avoid

conversation with Dad. He shut his eyes but too much was going through his mind and all he could do was pretend to be asleep. They had driven about five minutes when Dad turned on the radio. An oldies station came on. It was in the middle of a song but Kaden instantly recognized it and the lyrics made his stomach tighten up again. It was the song about needing trust and faith. The song also had a line about not making the same mistake twice. Kaden fought back the tears forming under his closed eyes but couldn't fight back the hurt of knowing his father was making the same mistake twice.

CHAPTER THIRTY-FIVE

IN TROUBLE

When Dad pulled into the circle driveway, Gram was waiting on the porch. Kaden saw her stand up and cross her arms. He knew that wasn't good.

Dad parked the truck between Cabins Four and Five and headed toward the porch like there wasn't a worry on his mind. Kaden slowly followed behind.

Gram waited until Dad was at the porch. Then she yelled to Kaden, "Stop acting like a guilty turtle and get up here, on the double!" Kaden sped up.

"Where have you two been?" Gram said. She said "two" but she was looking directly at Dad.

"It's only seven twenty," Dad said. "We dropped Yo-Yo off

right at seven and headed straight home."

"You told me he had to be home at six."

This wasn't what Kaden thought Gram would be mad about.

"Yo-Yo called his mom and she said he didn't have to be home until seven," Kaden said. He didn't feel like defending Dad but it was the truth.

Now Gram glared at Kaden. "So Yo-Yo called his mom, did he? I'm glad someone takes responsibility around here. Neither of you let me know about the time change. And what about you, Kaden? Why didn't you call Emmett?"

That was what Kaden had expected and he didn't have an excuse.

"I forgot," Kaden said quietly. "I'm sorry."

"You must have thought about it when you drove past his house. That fancy phone of yours doesn't work?"

"I forgot it, too. And Yo-Yo accidently left his phone on my desk and Dad said he forgot his, too. But I did ask Dad to stop," Kaden explained. The tears he fought back in the truck now streamed down his cheeks. "But he had already driven past and wouldn't turn around. I really am sorry, Gram, really."

"Sorry doesn't cut it," Gram said, but then turned her wrath back on Dad.

"And what's the matter with you? A grown man can't let bygones be bygones? What kind of example are you setting for that boy, refusing to let him at least try to be responsible?" Gram said. "You could have turned around."

"There are some bygones a man can't forget," Dad said. He turned his head and spat.

Gram turned silent. Like the calm before a storm, Kaden knew Gram was fuming.

"Go to your cabin, Kaden," Gram said flatly. "But first bring me those cell phones, both yours and Yo-Yo's. A phone is a tool and it takes responsibility to use tools."

Kaden walked to his cabin. His pillow was still on his desk. It seemed like years since Yo-Yo tossed it at him. Under the pillow were the two phones.

"I'll let you take Yo-Yo's back to him Monday when you go to school," Gram said as Kaden handed her the phones. "But I'll hang on to yours until you show me you know how to be responsible. Now, go on back to your cabin."

As he sat down on his bed Kaden heard Gram through the open window.

"Just where did you take those two all day?" Gram asked.

"We went to Amazon Amazement," Dad said. "I have the right to take my son to an amusement park if I want."

"You don't have the right to take him anywhere without

323

my permission and you know it," Gram stated. "I have total custody of that boy."

"Only while I was in prison."

"You're still on parole," Gram said. "I won't deny you access to your son but you still have to have my permission until your parole is over. Besides, I wasn't talking about doing something with Kaden. I was talking about taking responsibility. When are you going to start doing that?"

"When are you going to start trusting me?" Dad said.

"When you show you can be trustworthy," Gram stated, and that was it. Gram was done. Kaden heard the screen door open and close and then Gram's footsteps over the intercom. Through the window, he heard Dad go down the porch steps and head toward Cabin Five. Then the truck started and Kaden heard gravel scatter as it skidded out of the driveway.

Tears welled up in Kaden's eyes again and rolled quickly down his cheeks. This should have been the best day of his life. He had dreamed of days like this for years. He and his father, together like other sons and fathers, at someplace really awesome. Dad, Yo-Yo, Amazon Amazement. It had all the right ingredients for a perfect day. It should have been. But it wasn't. Instead, Kaden felt it was the worst day of his life.

Kaden wiped his eyes with the back of his hand and took

the carved lizard from his pocket. He looked it over carefully. A sharp ridge ran the length of its back, its tail curved like an S. It even had tiny toes. The wood was stained with brown spots and a tiny sliver of red felt stuck out the slit of its mouth for its tongue. Kaden wished he could carve like that. The lizard was beautiful. He turned it over and felt the smoothness of the lizard's belly, and then, with all his might, he hurled the lizard against the wall.

Sunday, September 18

CHAPTER THIRTY-SIX

CONFRONTATION

Kaden sat across the table from Gram, stirring his oatmeal. He hadn't taken a bite. Gram hadn't said a word to him. He felt terrible he had disappointed her. He felt ashamed he had let Emmett down. But he felt sick to his stomach when he thought about his dad.

Yesterday, all he wanted to do was get home without Dad buying anything else. But today, even though he was apprehensive, he knew he'd have to tell what happened. Someone would have to call the sheriff. But he just wasn't ready to face that.

"Is Dad here?" Kaden finally said.

"No, he didn't come back last night."

They sat in silence a while longer. Gram finished her oatmeal. Kaden stirred his.

"I'm sorry about yesterday," Kaden said, his eyes on his bowl.

"I know you are."

"Can I go to Emmett's? I need to apologize face-to-face."

"That's what I was waiting to hear," Gram said, "but you should wait until a little later. He might still be resting."

"Resting?" Emmett was like Gram, always up at the crack of dawn.

"Yes, he had a little accident," Gram said. "Emmett started splitting wood by himself—"

Kaden looked up in alarm and interrupted Gram. "Accident? Is he hurt? Why didn't you tell me last night?"

"Last night wasn't the time to talk about it. I had other things I needed to say to your father. But Emmett's okay. He was trying to stack too much wood on that rickety old trailer and it rolled off and fell on him. His leg has a big slash in it and he's pretty stoved up but he'll be all right. It could have been a lot worse."

"It's all my fault," Kaden said. "It wouldn't have happened if I had been there."

"No, it probably wouldn't have," Gram said, "but Emmett should have known not to start without you, too."

"How did you find out?" Kaden said.

"When he came here to get you, I was surprised he didn't know you were gone. I had no idea where you were either. We were both surprised you didn't call him. He said the wood would wait until today. But I had a feeling he'd go ahead without you, so I walked down to check on him after lunch. It was a good thing I did. He was pinned to the ground, all the wood on top of him."

Kaden still hadn't taken a bite and now tears were welling up in his eyes again. Gram sat there for a while, quietly watching him.

"Don't worry, he'll be fine as rain in a few days," Gram said. When Kaden didn't look up, Gram continued. "Is there something else on your mind other than not calling Emmett yesterday? Did something happen at the amusement park?"

Kaden continued staring into his oatmeal, slowly stirring it around and around.

"Yeah," he finally said, then looked up at Gram. "I'm going to tell you but I have to think things through first."

"That's fine," Gram said. "I've always told you to think first, not act on impulse. So eat up that oatmeal before you churn it to butter. Then maybe you should take a walk to the tower. Walking is good for thinking. And when you're ready, I'll be here to listen."

"Thanks, Gram, I know you will and I really am sorry," Kaden said. He slowly pushed his chair back and headed for the door but stopped and turned to face Gram.

"I love you," he said.

"I love you, too, Kaden," Gram said.

Kaden walked slowly down the road. When he reached the muddy spot, he couldn't tell if the tire tracks were old or new. As he got closer to the barricade, he was relieved to see Dad's truck was not there. But when he walked up the weedy path, he stopped short. Emmett's ladder leaned against the tower. Confused, Kaden stepped back out of sight. He wondered where Dad was. He doubted Dad would walk to the tower with the ladder and leave his truck elsewhere. But he wanted to be sure. He didn't want to meet up with him.

Kaden squinted at the tower. He couldn't see anyone in the windows. He wished when Yo-Yo gave him the periscope, he had come down to see what it looked like from below. They had talked about checking but never did it. Now he looked to see if he could spot it spying on him. He saw nothing unusual.

Then Kaden realized something else. Kubla hadn't made a sound. Kaden looked toward the limb. Kubla was sitting there preening himself. Kubla never did that when he was worried. Kaden stepped out into the open. As soon as he did, Kubla came darting from his limb and landed on his head.

He gurgled in Kaden's ear, totally unalarmed. Kubla was just as good as a watchdog. Kaden knew the tower was vacant.

Kubla gently tugged on Kaden's hair before he flapped his wings and jumped from his head. The crow flew to the crossbeam and waited as Kaden climbed the ladder to the landing. Then he flew to the top of the tower and disappeared through a window as Kaden climbed the rest of the way up.

Kaden held his breath as he poked his head up through the trapdoor. Dad was not there. The tower cabin looked the same as it always did except Dad's old sleeping bag was stretched out across the floor. Kubla stood on a jean jacket wadded up as a pillow.

"I guess Dad slept here last night, didn't he, Kubla?" Kaden said to the bird. "Did you get any sleep?"

Kubla partially opened his wings and jumped to the chest. Kaden stared at the lock. He was afraid of what he might find but he had to look. Kaden's heart beat fast as he dialed the combination and opened the lid. But nothing had been moved. Nothing added. Nothing taken.

Kaden picked up the cell phone from the chest and flipped it open and closed, open and closed, not really thinking about calling anyone. He knew it didn't work. But the phone made him think if he had only let Emmett know he was going to the amusement park, he wouldn't feel so ashamed of himself.

He knew he couldn't help his father's actions, but his own were totally his responsibility.

Without thinking, Kaden slipped the phone into his pocket and rummaged around the chest again until he found the rasp. He pushed the sleeping bag and jacket aside, sat down in the corner, and started scraping the walking stick he was making for Gram. Scraping and scraping, over and over, removing little bits of wood. Scraping felt good. He scraped harder. Kubla jumped into the open chest. Kaden heard him getting into the bag of sunflower seeds. He didn't mind. He kept scraping. The morning was warm but a cool breeze hinted of fall. He kept scraping. He pictured the carved lizard in his head and looked at the big knob of wood at the top of the stick, envisioning an intricately carved crow. He kept scraping.

The methodical rhythm of the rasp scraping over the wood was relaxing and let Kaden's mind wander. And it wandered all over the place. He thought about his earliest memories, when he didn't have a care in the world, and worried about now, when he knew what he was going to have to do. And all the while, Kaden just kept scraping, scraping, scraping.

Suddenly Kubla jumped to the window with a piercing caw. Kaden startled. From down below the tower, he heard his father.

"Kaden! Are you up there?"

Kaden didn't answer. He didn't get up. He kept scraping. Over the sounds of Kubla's insistent warning cries, Kaden heard his father call again. "Kaden, answer me!"

Kaden kept scraping. He heard his dad's footsteps on the ladder. Then he heard the sound of his dad stepping onto the landing, then a different sound as he climbed the stairs. The difference repeated itself over and over. Landing, stairs. Landing, stairs. Nine landings, thirteen stairs. Kaden kept scraping.

"Why didn't you answer me?" Dad demanded as his head came through the trapdoor. Kaden didn't look up. He just kept scraping. As his father climbed the last steps through the trapdoor, Kubla flew around outside the tower, cawing and cawing incessantly. Kaden kept scraping.

Dad walked over and grabbed Kaden's wrist in a hard grip. Kaden jerked his arm away and started scraping again. Dad grabbed the rasp and walking stick away from Kaden. He tossed the rasp down through the open trapdoor. It bounced down, making loud clanging noises, metal hitting metal as it hit stair after stair, until Kaden heard it thump on the ground. With the noises, Kubla's cawing quickened and grew sharper. Dad stood there looking at Kaden, his hand grasping the end of the walking stick, the knob of wood resting on the floor.

"What's the matter with you? So you got in a little trouble for not calling that old fool."

Kaden said nothing even though he felt his face redden. He wished he had the rasp and the walking stick back. It would be easier if his hands had something to do.

Kaden took a deep breath, looked straight at his father, and said, "Who's Michael Smith?"

"Michael Smith?" Dad said. "I don't know any Michael Smith. What are you talking about?"

"Well, you certainly know Emmett Adams," Kaden said, his eyes never leaving Dad's. "And I know you were using his credit card yesterday."

"He owes me. And if you open your mouth about that, you'll be sorry and so will Emmett," Dad said, viciously raising his voice. "That's a promise."

"No, that's a threat," Kaden said angrily. "I don't understand you. You didn't have to steal again. And why are you so angry at Emmett? What's he ever done to you anyway?"

"I never would have gone to prison if it weren't for that old snitch snooping around, then calling the sheriff. You think I should be buddy-buddy with the man who kept me from raising my son? Do you think I like hearing you talk about him like he's your father? All of it is Emmett's fault."

Gram had said it was best to think things through but

Kaden didn't need to think any longer this time. What he thought came out instinctively.

"No, you're wrong. Emmett didn't do anything," Kaden said, looking straight in his father's eyes. "You did. And you still are. You may be my father but you don't act like one. And you never have."

Kubla was still flying around and around, circling the outside of the tower, his cawing growing more and more raucous and high-pitched. Other crows were answering him with a confusing scramble of voices, like a pack of dogs all barking at different pitches, but sharper and more defined, more agitated. As if to direct the other birds to the tower, Kubla landed on the window frame and gave three ear-piercing screeches.

Kaden saw Dad lift the walking stick.

"No!" he screamed as Dad swung the stick like a baseball bat at the bird.

The big knob hit Kubla's side with a sickening thud. The bird was knocked off the window frame. Kaden sprang to the window. He saw Kubla try to open his wings. But Kubla couldn't turn out of this plummet and Kaden watched helplessly as the crow fell to the ground.

Kaden pushed past Dad and dropped through the trapdoor. It seemed like his legs were in slow motion. He couldn't make them move fast enough as he went down flight after flight of stairs. He finally reached the lowest landing and hurried down the ladder. He briefly looked up. Dad was not following after him but Kaden pulled the cord on the ladder. The top slid down and he let the ladder fall to the ground with a metallic crash as he rushed to Kubla's side.

Kubla lay motionless in the grass. One of his wings was bent backward. Kaden rubbed the bird's head. Kubla didn't move or make a sound but Kaden could tell he was looking at him. Kaden took off his shirt and spread it on the ground. Gently he smoothed Kubla's wing back to his side, picked up the bird, and put him on his shirt. Gingerly, he wrapped the shirt around the bird. Then, cradling Kubla like a baby, Kaden ran.

As he ran, the cell phone bounced against his leg. He stopped and took it out of his pocket. He looked at it for a second, then flipped it open. His hand shook as he pushed 9-1-1. A woman's voice came on the phone.

"What is your emergency?" she said.

With tears streaming down his face, Kaden said, "You need to send the sheriff to the fire tower."

CHAPTER THIRTY-SEVEN

FORGIVING

Kaden ran all the way down the dirt road. When he reached the main road, he turned left and ran down the hill. He was relieved to see Emmett's truck in the drive. The splitter sat in the grass beside the shop and the trailer was parked next to it. Split logs were scattered all around. Kaden ran to Emmett's door.

"Emmett! Emmett!" he yelled as he opened the door and rushed into the kitchen. Kaden could hear the TV. He raced into the living room. Emmett sat in his recliner, feet up, looking toward the television. A large bandage was taped to his shin.

"So you finally showed up," Emmett said, not turning to

look at Kaden.

Kaden had stopped crying as he ran but now he burst into tears. Emmett turned around and saw Kaden standing there, holding a bundle in his arms. Blood seeped through the shirt.

Emmett jumped up, moaning as he did. "What happened? Are you okay?"

"It's Kubla." His words were barely audible. He opened the bundle. Emmett looked closely at the bird and put his fingers to Kubla's throat.

"He's still alive," he said, gently taking the bird from Kaden. "Let's get him to the vet. Go grab one of my shirts. You can tell me about it in the truck."

As Kaden dashed to Emmett's room, he heard Emmett opening and closing kitchen drawers.

"Now, where is my wallet?" Emmett said to himself. Kaden came into the kitchen wearing one of the man's T-shirts. Letting Emmett keep on searching, he reached for the kitchen phone.

"Gram, I don't have time to explain but I'm going with Emmett," Kaden blurted out. "Kubla's been hurt and we have to take him to the vet. And there's something else, too. Dad's at the tower and the sheriff will be coming."

Amazed at what he was hearing, Emmett had stopped

searching. He stood frozen in place, staring at Kaden.

Kaden paused, listening. "No, I'm fine, Gram. I'll tell you all about it later. We have to hurry." Before Kaden hung up, he added one more thing. "Oh, and Gram, lock your door until the sheriff gets there."

On the way to Chapston City, Kaden held Kubla on his lap. The crow was bundled up to keep him warm but Kaden opened the shirt enough to stroke his head with his finger. He put his head close to Kubla's and gurgled to the bird, a comforting gurgle, the gurgle made between friends. And as they drove, Kaden told Emmett everything that had happened since the hot dog cookout.

"What's really confusing," Kaden said, "is I had fun with Dad sometimes and thought . . . I don't know what I thought. Sometimes I liked him and I thought he liked me. Other times I didn't like him at all and I thought he hated me. I thought he was going to do better, but he didn't. He didn't even try."

"Life is complex," Emmett said. "You can like someone, you can even love someone, but still not like the way he behaves, still not agree with him or see eye to eye."

"Well, I hate him for what he did to Kubla. I can't

forgive that."

"Sometimes, things are hard to forgive," Emmett said.

Kaden was quiet for a few minutes.

"What didn't you forgive Dad for?" he finally said.

"For deserting his son," Emmett said. "He could have chosen differently and been there for you all along. That was totally his decision. When you decide to take an action, you also decide to take the consequences."

Kaden sat stroking Kubla. There was one thing he had left out about what happened at the tower. One thing he hadn't told Emmett.

"Up in the tower, Dad told me you called the sheriff on him. Is that true?"

"Yes," Emmett said. "It was the hardest thing I ever had to do, to turn in the son of my best friend. But it was the rightest thing I ever did, too. I know that and I've forgiven myself for it."

"It wasn't to get even for Kubla that I called the sheriff. I had already decided to do that."

Kaden stopped stroking Kubla and looked over at Emmett. "Do you think Dad will be able to forgive me?"

"I don't know," Emmett said. "I hope so, but I don't know."

At the veterinary clinic Kaden handed Kubla to a nurse, who took him into a back room. Kaden and Emmett sat in the waiting room.

"I'm sorry about yesterday," Kaden said. "I got all excited and forgot to call before we left."

"I understand the situation and you're forgiven," Emmett said. "But just remember, a man is only as good as his word."

"I won't forget," Kaden said.

The door opened and the vet came out. He was holding Kubla's small body wrapped in clean cloths. He handed the bundle to Kaden and shook his head.

Monday, September 19

CHAPTER THIRTY-EIGHT

A NEW DAY

When Kaden awoke the next morning, he thought it was really early. His cabin was dark like it would be just before sunrise. As he rolled over, he remembered all that happened the day before but no more tears came to his eyes. Kaden felt all cried out but still didn't want to face the day. He let out a long sigh. Gram's voice instantly came over the intercom.

"You finally awake?"

Kaden looked at his clock. Nine thirty-seven. Confused, he rubbed his eyes and looked at the clock again. Still 9:37. He sat up in bed. Gram had closed the solid wood door and had also closed his curtains. No wonder it was so dark.

"I overslept," Kaden said. "Why didn't you wake me up?

I've already missed first period."

"You needed the sleep," Gram said. "I sent a note with Doris telling the school you'd be absent today. I gave her Yo-Yo's phone, too. She'll take it to him."

"Why didn't you just call the school?" Kaden asked.

"A note works just as well and you can say what you want without interruption or questions," Gram stated. "Get dressed and I'll fix you some oatmeal."

"I'm going to take a shower first," Kaden said.

When Kaden got to Cabin Four, his heart lurched. Dad's truck was parked between Cabins Four and Five. Kaden rushed to Gram's cabin.

"I think Dad's back," he said in a panicked voice. "His truck's out there."

"No, don't worry. He's not here," Gram said. "Yesterday morning, after you went to the tower, your dad came back saying he wanted to talk with you. I told him where you were and he walked to the tower. The truck was here yesterday when Emmett brought you home but you were so upset you just didn't notice it. The sheriff will be coming this afternoon with a tow truck. He wants to talk with you, too."

"A tow truck?" Kaden asked.

"Yes, the truck was stolen, too. Belonged to some kid going to college who left the keys under the seat. The sheriff

347

will take the truck and all the stuff in it. He'll have to take the gifts your dad gave us, too. He used stolen credit cards for everything. All the stuff, including the wallets and credit cards, will be used as evidence and then returned to their rightful owners."

Kaden walked over to the kitchen table. There was a large paper bag on it. He looked inside. In it were all his belongings from the tower but the only item he focused on was a box of matchsticks. Kaden slumped down into a chair, put his elbows on the table and his head in his hands. He had thought he had cried all he could but now he couldn't keep tears from dropping onto the yellow plastic tablecloth.

"Your dad told the sheriff the things in the tower weren't stolen, they belonged to you. The sheriff left them here yesterday."

When Kaden didn't look up, Gram put her hand on his shoulder.

"I know it hurts to think about Kubla," Gram said. She paused for a long moment before continuing. "I also know you're disappointed in your father. I am, too. From the first time I talked with him, I was worried he'd go back to his old ways but I hoped with all my heart that he wouldn't. I know you were hoping for better, too."

Kaden wiped his eyes and looked up at his grandmother.

He could tell from her face she hurt as much as he did.

"It will be hard for a while," Gram continued. "I'm not going to lie to you. But you did the right thing. I want you to remember that."

"I know," Kaden said, "but knowing something doesn't make it any easier."

"No," Gram said, giving his shoulder a squeeze, "but we'll get through this."

After breakfast Kaden walked to the tower, carrying a shovel and Kubla's body wrapped in the cloths. He buried Kubla under the tree where the shadow of the bird's favorite limb stretched across the ground. Then he went into the weeds to collect the friendship rock and rope. They were the only things that weren't in the bag the sheriff left.

Back at his cabin, Kaden took a piece of plywood. He thickly spread glue all over it. Then on the board, Kaden looped the rope into the shape of a large crow. Still attached to the rope, the friendship rock sat under the bird as if the bird were standing on it. Kaden went to the bag on his bed and pulled out the box of matches. He took out a matchstick and glued it to the rope beak. When the glue dried, he would walk back to the tower and leave it as a headstone at Kubla's grave.

Kaden emptied the rest of the paper bag on his bed. He was putting the binoculars on his dresser when suddenly the sound of guitars and drums came through the intercom. In a second, several trumpets joined in. Kaden looked at his clock. It was exactly five minutes after the last class ended at school. Gram's voice came over the intercom.

"Your cell phone is making a racket," she stated.

"It's Yo-Yo calling," Kaden said. "He downloaded that ringtone for me so I would know who's calling." The song was repeating for the third time.

"Well, you better come answer it," Gram said.

Surprised at Gram's statement, Kaden ran from his cabin. The song had stopped playing by the time he got in Gram's door.

"I can call him back," Kaden said as he reached up and got the phone Gram had put on top of the refrigerator Saturday night. When he turned around, Gram held her hand out, empty palm up.

"Give it to me," she said.

Confused, Kaden put the phone in her palm. Gram put the phone on the table beside the backpack, glove, ball, MP3 player, and TV remote. Then she went into her bedroom.

Kaden heard her dresser drawer open and close. Soon Gram returned to the living room. She had another phone in her hand.

"You'll have to give that one to the sheriff when he gets here," Gram said. "Have Yo-Yo put his song on this one." She handed her phone to Kaden. "I don't want a phone, but you do."

"Thanks, Gram," Kaden said. He gave her a quick peck on the cheek, then raced back to his cabin. When he sat down at his desk, something didn't seem right. At first, Kaden couldn't put his finger on it but then it dawned on him. He couldn't hear Gram in her cabin. Not her humming, not her footsteps, not even the sound of her fan. Kaden looked at the intercoms. Neither of the little red lights was lit up. Gram had turned off both intercoms.

Kaden started to punch in Yo-Yo's number but then he stopped and hung up. He would call Yo-Yo later and tell him all about what had happened. But first he had another call to make. Kaden pushed the number and put the phone to his ear.

"Emmett," Kaden said, "do you need any help?"

JUDY YOUNG

Judy Young is the award-winning author of eighteen picture books, including *R is for Rhyme: A Poetry Alphabet* (Mom's Choice Gold Recipient); *A Book for Black-Eyed Susan* (WILLA Literary Award Finalist and NAPPA Gold Recipient); and *A Pet for Miss Wright* (IRA-CBC Children's Choice List). She resides in the foothills of the Bear River Range near Mink Creek, Idaho, with her husband, Ross, who once befriended a crow he named Kubla. Kubla often sat on Judy's shoulder, pecked at her hair, and gurgled into her ear, possibly instilling ideas and inspiration for *Promise*, Judy's first novel. Visit Judy at www.judyyoungpoetry.com.